"Well—" said Pierce, clearing his throat "—would you like to have your first swimming lesson right now?"

The edginess that had infected him must have been contagious. Amy's head bobbed, and her intriguing brown gaze turned aside momentarily. Finally, her eyes lifted to his as she answered with a tiny nod.

The timidity she exhibited did something strange to the air surrounding him. Even though he was standing waist-deep in the bay, he felt flushed, overheated.

She looked the very essence of freshness. Of vitality. And until this very instant, he'd never realized how her energy enthralled him. His heart tripped against his ribs as he realized that in order to teach Amy to swim, he was going to have to get close to her—*very* close.

Dear Reader,

Discover a guilt-free way to enjoy this holiday season. Treat yourself to four calorie-free, but oh-so-satisfying brand-new Silhouette Romance titles this month.

Start with *Santa Brought a Son* (#1698) by Melissa McClone. This heartwarming reunion romance is the fourth book in Silhouette Romance's new six-book continuity, MARRYING THE BOSS'S DAUGHTER.

Would a duty-bound prince forsake tradition to marry an enchanting commoner? Find out in *The Prince & the Marriage Pact* (#1699), the latest episode in THE CARRAMER TRUST miniseries by reader favorite Valerie Parv.

Then, it's anyone's guess if a wacky survival challenge can end happily ever after. Join the fun as the romantic winners of a crazy contest are revealed in *The Bachelor's Dare* (#1700) by Shirley Jump.

And in Donna Clayton's *The Nanny's Plan* (#1701), a would-be sophisticate is put through the ringer by a drop-dead gorgeous, absentminded professor and his rascally twin nephews.

So pick a cozy spot, relax and enjoy all four of these tender holiday confections that Silhouette Romance has cooked up just for you.

Happy holidays!

Mavis C. Allen
Associate Senior Editor

Please address questions and book requests to:
Silhouette Reader Service
U.S.: 3010 Walden Ave., P.O. Box 1325, Buffalo, NY 14269
Canadian: P.O. Box 609, Fort Erie, Ont. L2A 5X3

The Nanny's Plan

DONNA CLAYTON

SILHOUETTE *Romance*®

Published by Silhouette Books

America's Publisher of Contemporary Romance

This book is lovingly dedicated to
Mrs. Margaret Edwards, the third-grade teacher
who sparked my lifelong love of books
by introducing me to Beverly Cleary.

 SILHOUETTE BOOKS

ISBN 0-373-19701-2

THE NANNY'S PLAN

Visit Silhouette at www.eHarlequin.com

Printed in U.S.A.

Books by Donna Clayton

Silhouette Romance

Mountain Laurel #720
Taking Love in Stride #781
Return of the Runaway Bride #999
Wife for a While #1039
Nanny and the Professor #1066
Fortune's Bride #1118
Daddy Down the Aisle #1162
**Miss Maxwell Becomes
   a Mom* #1211
*Nanny in the Nick of Time #1217
**Beauty and the Bachelor
   Dad* #1223
*†The Stand-By Significant
   Other* #1284
*†Who's the Father of Jenny's
   Baby?* #1302

The Boss and the Beauty #1342
His Ten-Year-Old Secret #1373
Her Dream Come True #1399
Adopted Dad #1417
His Wild Young Bride #1441
**The Nanny Proposal #1477
***The Doctor's Medicine
   Woman* #1483
**Rachel and the M.D. #1489
Who Will Father My Baby? #1507
In Pursuit of a Princess #1582
*††The Sheriff's 6-Year-Old
   Secret* #1623
*††The Doctor's Pregnant
   Proposal* #1635
††Thunder in the Night #1647
The Nanny's Plan #1701

Silhouette Books

The Coltons
Close Proximity

*The Single Daddy Club
†Mother & Child
**Single Doctor Dads
††The Thunder Clan

DONNA CLAYTON

is the recipient of the Diamond Author Award For Literary Achievement 2000 as well as two HOLT Medallions. In her opinion, love *is* what makes the world go 'round. She takes great pride in knowing that, through her work, she provides her readers the chance to indulge in some purely selfish romantic entertainment.

One of her favorite pastimes is traveling. Her other interests include walking, reading, visiting with friends, teaching Sunday school, cooking and baking, and she still collects cookbooks, too. In fact, her house is overrun with them.

Please write to Donna c/o Silhouette Books. She'd love to hear from you!

Dear Mom & Dad,

We are having fun this summer wit Uncle Pierce. We were worryed at furst becuz Uncle Pierce doesn't have any kidz & he doesn't really no how to have fun & he works to ~~mush~~ much! But the new nanny is fixing that. Amy keeps us buzy every day. She helped us bake the cookies four this care pakage. Yummy chocklit chips! Our favrite! We ate a few, but maled you most of them.

We are afraid that Uncle Pierce & Amy are ~~cu~~ coming down with some kind of straynge ~~dize di~~ getting sick. They keep looking at each other with funny goo-goo eyes like how youz look at each other befour you send us to watch movies on kidz nite and cloze your bedroom door. We dont no what is going on, but if they start runing a fever, we will call the ~~dokter~~ doctor.

Hope you are having a good time in Africa! don't wory about us! We are *fine!!* But we are not so sure about Uncle Pierce & the nanny.

With love from your ~~suns~~ sons,

Benjamin & Jeremiah

Chapter One

Amy Edwards had spent her whole life avoiding the traps: relationships, love, marriage and, most of all, kids. So why had she agreed to spend the summer caring for a set of six-year-old twins?

The only answer she could come up with was that she'd totally lost her mind.

She chuckled as she cut the engine. "Imagine that," she murmured, pulling the key from the ignition and opening the car door. "Temporary insanity made me a temporary nanny."

Because an inner ear infection had caused the airline's company physician to ground her for two months from her new job as a flight attendant, all she'd have been doing was watching the corn grow in Kansas while she waited to heal. And the pay offered to her had been generous.

Still... *taking care of children.*

If anyone other than her father had asked this of

her, she'd have turned them down flat. But she'd have crawled to the top of Mount Everest on her hands and knees for her dad. The good Lord knew he'd sure sacrificed for her.

She pulled her suitcase from the trunk and lifted her gaze. The stone-and-stucco house looked like something right out of the pages of a glossy architectural magazine. The vast grounds were neatly manicured, and flowers bloomed in a riot of color. The blue-green water of the Delaware Bay served as a tranquil backdrop to the setting. Even the idea of minding children couldn't dampen the bright prospect of spending eight weeks in this paradise.

Giddiness churned in her belly, urging her to go and take a quick peek at the cove. She should fight this feeling. This overzealousness that swallowed her up since escaping the Midwest made her feel so... small town. So unrefined. But before a few short weeks ago, she'd never seen a body of water larger than the man-made fishing pond just outside Lebo. The Delaware Bay was out there just waiting for her to feast her eyes on the view. Veering off the path that wound its way to the front door, she made a beeline for the water.

She heard the young voices before actually spotting the boys. Her charges, she quickly surmised. Two peas in a pod. Or rather, in a rowboat. They bobbed on the surface of the bay just offshore. She frowned and searched the area for whoever was supposed to be with them. Young children and deep water didn't mix well, in her mind.

"Jeremiah!" she called, lifting her hand in friendly greeting. "Benjamin!"

When the boys' mother had flown to Kansas to reacquaint herself with Amy, the woman had been clear that Benjamin was called Benjamin. Not Ben. Not Benny. But Benjamin.

The twins seemed startled by Amy's appearance; however, they tentatively returned her wave. She realized then that one of the boys had been crying.

She dropped her case to the grass. "What are you guys doing out there?"

It was impossible to tell one boy from the other, so she had no idea who it was who tipped his chin up defiantly and said, "We're going east. We're rowing out into the Atlantic Ocean."

Amy's mind raced. She quelled the urge to shout at them to return to shore this instant. Instead, she thought it better to make friends and coax the boys to safety.

"I'm not an expert in geography," she told them amiably. "But I'm pretty sure that, if you head due east, you're going to run smack into New Jersey."

The boys looked surprised by this news.

Before they could regroup, Amy called, "How about if you come ashore and we'll go inside to check the atlas and you can see for yourself where you are."

The child with the red-rimmed eyes stood up, clearly impatient with her suggestion, at the same time stating, "We know where *we* are."

Panic made Amy's tone grow more stern. "Sit down. Right now."

The boat was hit with a gentle wave that sent it rocking, and both boys' eyes widened in alarm. An oar slipped from its ring, momentum sending it bobbing several feet from the boat.

"I'm coming." Without thought, Amy slipped off her high-heeled shoes and started toward them. She hoped the water wasn't too deep. Swimming wasn't much of a concern in Kansas, where you were surrounded by farmland.

The bay was cold, despite the clear, sunny sky overhead. Her skin broke out in goose bumps when the water reached waist level, and she shivered. She was nearly within arm's reach of the rowboat when the thought passed through her mind that the twins had gone oddly silent. That's when she heard a masculine voice behind her say, "Maybe this will help."

She twisted around just as her hand closed over the wooden bow.

Sunlight gilded the man's jet-black hair, sparked the greenest gaze in all the universe. The honed angles comprising his features made for an utterly handsome face. A breath-stealing face.

Amy gaped.

Inexorably, she slowly became aware that the gorgeous man standing on the shore had a rope in his hand. Her gaze followed the dripping line, and her cheeks burned with embarrassment when she realized that one end was tethered to the front of the rowboat.

"Jeremiah," the man said, "sit down."

The child obeyed. The boat swayed under her grasp.

"Hold on," he told the twins. "I'm going to haul you in."

Out of the corner of her eye she spied the oar. She waded toward it, and when her fingers curled around the smooth surface, she was struck with the realization that the salty bay water had surely ruined her silk shirtdress. She was going to look a wreck when she trudged ashore.

Confidence. She must remember to don an air of self-assurance. Her instructor at flight attendant school had been adamant—perception was everything. If a traveler sensed you were calm and in control during any given situation, then the battle was nearly won.

She slogged onto the sand, the fabric of her dress sticking to her thighs as if it had been glued on.

The man had pulled the bow of the boat onto dry land and was plucking the boys from it when he said to her, "You're Amy Edwards? The nanny?"

"Yes. That would be me." She stepped forward meaning to offer him her hand, but realized her fingers were cold and damp, so she eased them behind her back. "You're Dr. Kincaid. The boys' uncle."

Her well-practiced, cocksure tone came without thought, but she was anything but certain. The boys' parents had been scheduled to leave before she arrived in Glory, Delaware. But for all Amy knew, plans could have changed. Cynthia Winthrop had told her that her brother would be with the boys when Amy arrived; however, the man could be anyone—another relative, a family friend, a neighbor.

He smiled, and Amy's brain went haywire. She felt as if she might melt right into the carpet of thick grass beneath her bare feet.

"That's right," he told her. "Call me Pierce."

He crouched down on his haunches then, turning his attention to the children.

"I thought I left you in front of the television

watching a video," he said, a distinct reprimand in his tone.

"But the movie's been over for a long time, Uncle Pierce," one of the boys complained.

"A long time," the other parroted.

Surprise lifted his features. He studied his wristwatch. Then his shoulders rounded a bit and he looked down at his nephews. "So it has. I'm sorry, boys. I guess I got caught up in my work."

Once again that vivid green gaze was on her, and it unsettled her all over again. She fought the urge to smooth her hand over her soggy dress.

"I have to say," he told her, placing his palms on his knees and standing, "I'm impressed with your quick attempt to fetch the boys. Although I find it amusing that you went at the rescue the hard way. The lanyard was lying right there."

Her heart pounded. Explaining herself wasn't something she did very well, especially when she felt put on the spot. Her father had warned her that Dr. Pierce Kincaid was a highly intelligent man...and Amy usually avoided highly intelligent men. For very good reason. However, neither her dad nor Cynthia Winthrop had warned Amy that the doctor could be a grumpy Gus when he wanted to be.

During her two-day drive from Kansas, she'd pondered a hundred possible situations that might leave her looking like an idiot in front of the doctor, as well as means to avoid them. Walking into the Delaware Bay, fully clothed, had not been a scenario she'd anticipated.

"How could I see it?" she asked when the idea

came to her like a bolt from the blue. "It was under water until you picked it up."

The man's oh-so-perfect mouth went flat. He murmured, "I guess that's true enough."

She added, "Besides that, someone had to rescue the oar."

He nodded, his features relaxing as he looked at her.

"They shouldn't have been out here alone." She hadn't meant to criticize, but the opinion seemed to roll off her tongue by its own volition.

Contrition darkened his green gaze. "You're absolutely right. I shouldn't have lost track of time like that." After a moment, he sighed and then focused his attention on the twins.

"What were the two of you thinking?"

"The boat wasn't on the list of rules you gave us," one child quickly replied, blatant defensiveness in his tone. "So we thought it would be okay."

One of the man's dark eyebrows arched dubiously. "Obviously your powers of deduction haven't fully matured."

The second twin said, "It was Benjamin's idea."

"Was not!"

"Was too!"

"Boys."

Although his voice hadn't risen at all, the children went quiet. Amy chuckled.

Horrified that all eyes were on her, she reached up and pressed her fingers to her mouth. It was nerves. No doubt about it. This situation had her as tense as a lop-eared rabbit in a rocking-chair factory.

"I'm sorry," she said. Unwilling to reveal her state

of anxiety, she only shrugged. "The twins sure are cute when they squabble."

One corner of his mouth turned up. "They're cuter when they're not getting into trouble."

Automatically Amy's gaze drifted to the twins. The red, bleary eyes of one, the defiant chin thrust of the other. A strange thing happened to her insides. They turned all warm and mushy.

"You said you were heading east," she said. "Out into the Atlantic. You were going after your mom and dad, weren't you? You were heading for Africa."

The child who had been crying blinked, his chin trembling at the mention of his parents, and Amy thought her heart would dissolve right there in her chest.

She went to him, bent down and tilted her head to one side. His cheek was downy soft against her fingertips. "Are you Jeremiah? Or Benjamin?"

"Jeremiah." The child could barely speak around the emotion lumping in his throat.

"Well, Jeremiah, I know how you're feeling. I miss my parents, too."

He sniffed. "Did *your* mom and dad go to Africa?"

Her mouth curled. "No. My dad is back in Kansas." She paused, not quite knowing how to explain about her mother. "My mom went far, far away."

"Farther than Africa?" Benjamin's tone was awed.

"Farther than Africa." She gave both boys a smile. "But you know what I do when I'm missing them something fierce?"

The children waited, subdued anticipation holding them still.

"I keep busy doing fun things," she told him. Then she grinned. "And that's just what we're going to do this summer. You and me. Lots of fun things."

"Speaking of fun things," the boys' uncle interjected, "who's ready for dinner?"

She straightened and saw that he'd picked up the suitcase she'd left on the grass. He'd also gathered up her shoes. Having him carry her shoes felt too...personal to Amy. She hurried to take them from him. Their gazes collided and she murmured her appreciation. For a moment it seemed as if the cool breeze died and the sun grew hotter. Amy found it difficult to swallow.

But the stillness was broken when Jeremiah got upset all over again. He wailed, "But I don't like ruffled sprouts."

Benjamin's nose wrinkled. "They smell bad."

"They're Brussels sprouts." Pierce corrected his nephew with a laugh. "And they're good for you. Packed full of vitamins. If you don't like them, you don't have to eat them. All I ask is that you try them."

The boys trudged ahead of them toward the house, grumbling a warning that they intended to try only one, and that their uncle would know they didn't like it by all the gagging they would surely make.

Beside her, Pierce sighed. "I should have set an alarm clock or something. I shouldn't have left them alone for so long."

"You've got your work," Amy said. "When Mrs. Winthrop flew out to meet with me last week, she stressed that you had just been offered some kind of

special contract. That you were on a pressing dead-
line. It's understandable that—"

"But the boys could have been hurt."

Guilt seemed to pulse from him.

"I'm sorry there was a time lag between the boys'
parents' departure," Amy felt compelled to say, "and
my arriving. But it really couldn't be helped." She
lifted one shoulder. "I'm unable to fly."

"Yes. Cynthia told me that you'd been grounded."

Amy pointed to the side of her head. "It's an inner
ear thing. I'm not in any pain. Can't even tell there's
anything wrong. But the company physician refused
to risk a perforated eardrum that might be caused by
in-flight pressure changes."

"I see."

Silence fell like a lead balloon. Her bare feet made
her feel oddly vulnerable, but she didn't want to ruin
her shoes by putting them on when salt water was
still dripping down her legs from the hem of her dress.
She wondered if he noticed the faint but tangy odor
of the bay emanating from her. She really was a mess.

"Do you have experience with children?"

"What?" The question startled her. "No, I don't.
But your sister thought I'd do okay with the boys."

"This isn't an interview," he quickly assured her.
"I'm not questioning your skills."

Maybe not, but he was probing for information that
would cause him to form opinions about her. It was
her habit to avoid talking about herself as much as
possible. There were certain facts about herself she'd
rather no one discovered.

"It's just that you were so good with them," he

continued. "With Jeremiah especially. He's been pretty miserable since Cynthia and John left."

The slate stones of the patio were cool and smooth under the damp soles of her feet.

"Well, it's easy to imagine how he's feeling." She moistened her lips, shifted her shoes to her other hand. "Anyone who's hurting deserves a little compassion."

"It eases my mind to know that you would reach out to him like you did."

That odd stillness descended on them again, that strange heating up of the temperature, although Amy knew that was impossible.

"You must be exhausted," he said, his voice feather soft. "You've been driving for two days. I'll show you to your room so you can freshen up."

He slid open the French door through which the boys had already disappeared and motioned for her to enter before him.

"But I'm wet," she said, eyeing the carpet. "I'll ruin—"

"It's okay. Go on in."

The cream-colored rug felt luxuriously thick as she stepped inside on tiptoes.

"And don't worry if you don't make it down to eat with us," he told her, closing the door behind them. "Take your time freshening up. I'll keep a plate warm for you."

Just then they heard what sounded like a chair being dragged across the kitchen floor, then a loud thump, then the murmur of children's voices.

"Why don't you let me find my room by myself,"

she suggested. "It sounds like the boys might be getting…hungry."

"It does, doesn't it? They are a handful. Go up the back stairs there—" he pointed the way "—and your room is the yellow one just to the right. You can't miss it. Oh, and maybe later, after things quiet down, the two of us can meet in my study and discuss our schedules over a glass of wine. You'll need some time off. We can figure out which days you'll have free."

"That sounds good," she told him.

He started off toward the kitchen.

"Excuse me," she called.

He turned to face her.

"Um, I will need my suitcase."

"Oh, of course." He brought her the case with a murmured apology. "Sorry about that."

A grin that sexy should be deemed illegal, and his absentmindedness made him less formidable. It made him quite appealing, in fact.

She was smiling when he started off again. She couldn't help but call out his name a final time. From the expression on his face when he looked at her, it was clear he was baffled by what else could have slipped his mind.

"I just wanted to tell you that I like ruffled sprouts."

There was absolutely no logical reason for the odd feelings pulsing through Pierce. No logical reason whatsoever. He sat at his desk worrying his chin between his index finger and thumb.

He'd taken great care planning this room when he'd had the house built. With its floor-to-ceiling bookcases, the long oak conference table, the reading nook and the wall of wide windows, his study doubled as a library. A place he could feel comfortable reading, deciphering the data of his research and writing up his scientific findings. This richly paneled room was his oasis.

However, tonight he was finding no solace here.

"Amy Edwards is a great girl," his sister had told him. "She's unassuming and, well…very sweet. She'll be great with the boys, and you'll like her, I'm sure."

Cynthia had explained that for years Amy's father had owned a small motel just off the intrastate in Kansas. Amy had helped run the business. Cynthia and John had gotten to know the family while John had been the pastor of a small church in Lebo earlier in his career.

"She's honest and trustworthy," Cynthia had said, "and she's got a great work ethic."

His brother-in-law had added, "From what I remember, she was a mousy little thing."

Unassuming. Mousy. For some odd reason, those were the two adjectives that had stuck with him when he'd agreed to have the nanny in his home.

Pierce had always thought unassuming meant ordinary. And there was nothing ordinary about Amy Edwards. There was nothing mousy about her, either. She was the epitome of aplomb from the top of her coiffed head to the scarlet-painted tips of her toes…and they were very dainty toes, at that.

A scowl had his facial muscles tensing. He shouldn't be noticing Amy's bare toes. Or any of her other physical attributes, either. Like those shapely calves and thighs, and that nicely curved fanny.

But the wet silk had clung to her like the skin on a ripe plum. The sight had been just as enticing as a juicy piece of fruit, too, and he'd ended up feeling like a man who'd been starved for that particular food group.

His frowned deepened. He pushed himself from the chair and stalked to the window. What had gotten into him?

The reason he'd been so discombobulated by the woman, he guessed, was that he'd been expecting a plain Jane...but what had arrived was a stunning Stella. However, there had been more to it than merely her looks.

From his sister's accounting, Pierce had imagined Amy would be an average, regular, normal young woman—a barely grown kid, really, from the way Cynthia had described her. But the woman he'd seen when he'd gone down to the water's edge was polished and professional. Even standing up to her waist in the bay, she'd exuded a calm, no-nonsense air. When he'd questioned her methods of rescuing his nephews, she'd been quick to fire back a logical explanation that had exonerated her of any unsound decisions.

Although Pierce wouldn't have admitted this to anyone, he'd been a tad intimidated by the magnitude of her poise. He couldn't be sure, but at one point he suspected she'd actually chuckled at his handling of the whole situation. Of course, she'd explained away her sudden humor by expressing how cute the boys were, so his suspicion that she'd been laughing at his expense could be all in his head...

The knock on his study door made him turn. Amy stood at the threshold wearing a gold blouse that set off her rich brown eyes. Her skirt was short enough to show off her perfect knees. Her feet were clad in high heels that accentuated her narrow ankles and shapely calves. His gaze rose to her face, and when he noticed that her light brown hair was still swept up off her shoulders, he couldn't help but wonder how long it was and what it might look like in a tumble.

His mind was suddenly besieged with the image of him pulling the pins free himself, combing his fingers through those dark tresses. His gut tightened.

"Come in," he said, doing his damnedest to shove the alluring picture from his head.

"Is this a good time?" She entered the room, her shoulders square, her head high.

"Yes," he told her. "Have a seat. Would you like a glass of wine?"

Amy smiled. "That would be nice, thanks."

He went to the bar cabinet to pour their drinks. "I played a board game with the boys after dinner, gave them their baths and then tucked them into bed. They're settled for the night."

When he handed her the glass of merlot, he said, "They're in the room next door to you, by the way."

She took a sip, swallowed and then gazed off for a second. When she looked at him again her expression glowed with pleasure. "Delicious," she said, then her tongue smoothed over her lips.

Something happened down low in his belly. An odd fiery sensation sprouted to life.

"I'm ready to take over responsibility of the boys tomorrow morning."

She shifted in the seat, and Pierce was aware of the swish of her skirt fabric against the leather couch cushion. When she crossed her legs, the whisper of flesh against flesh had his breath stilling in his throat.

It was silly, really, this sudden fascination he found with that sound.

He took a drink—and a deep breath—desperate to clear this strange fog from his head.

"I'd like to gently recommend," he began, his gaze traveling down the length of her, "a change in your wardrobe."

A tiny crease appeared between her deep-set eyes.

"What I mean is," he rushed to explain, "Benjamin and Jeremiah are rambunctious boys. They run and jump and dig in the dirt and heaven only knows what else they'll have you doing."

"I see." Her smile was easy as she evidently realized he was only offering some friendly advice. "So I guess I'd be better off in pants."

"Exactly."

The tension in the room seemed to slacken then and the two of them spent some time talking about their situation—his work schedule and hers, and what each expected of the other.

As he refilled her glass, she commented, "This is a wonderful thing you're doing, letting the boys stay here. When Mrs. Winthrop and I met in Lebo, she was so excited about this trip to Africa."

Pierce topped off his own glass and then set the bottle on the marble-topped side table. His mouth screwed up in a grimace as he admitted, "I turned down her request at first."

"Oh?"

He eased himself back into the chair. "Yes. Cynthia came to me to explain that John had been offered the opportunity of his career. Six weeks as a missionary in Africa. Having the chance to do missionary work has always been my brother-in-law's dream, she said. She asked if I'd keep the boys for eight weeks, as the position required two weeks of studying the language and customs. I gently but firmly refused."

Pierce chuckled, remembering his well-reasoned denial.

"I reminded her," he continued, "that I wasn't the one who'd pined for hearth and home. That had been her. That I wasn't the one who'd been certain that parenthood would be the experience of a lifetime. That, too, had been her. And besides that, as she explained to you, I was just about to land a huge contract with one of the largest perfumeries in France. I couldn't afford to be away from the lab, away from my work…not for a single week, let alone two months.

"Cynthia seemed to understand." His smile widened. "But my sister is pretty stubborn. And it wasn't long before she returned with a whole new plan. A plan that involved you. She made it all sound so…workable. In the end, I agreed to take my nephews for the summer. As long as you were here to look after them during my working hours."

Amy set her empty glass on the table. "A reluctant hero is still a hero in my book."

Pierce had never thought of himself as a hero, reluctant or otherwise. The very idea unsettled him. He didn't know what to say, so he didn't say anything. The atmosphere stiffened up.

A few moments passed, and she stood. "I think I should head off to bed. If those boys are as rambunctious as you say, then I'm going to need a good night's sleep."

Her tapered fingers shot out and she tipped up her chin, and it took him a second to realize that she wanted to shake his hand. He stood and slid his palm into hers.

Her skin was warm against his. Smooth. And soft.

It was as if his every thought *gurgled* right out of his head.

"I want to assure you that I plan to do a good job," she proclaimed, giving his hand several good pumps. "We won't interrupt your work. In fact, when I'm with the boys you won't even know we're here."

Even though his gaze was riveted on the gentle sway of her bottom as she left his study, he did have enough of his wits about him to doubt her promise.

You won't even know we're here.

Her words echoed in his head. But he had serious doubts that he could be oblivious to the fact that Amy Edwards had invaded his home.

Chapter Two

"I'm so glad you told me about that tiny scar on your chin, Jeremiah," Amy said as she combed the child's hair neatly into place.

"It's the only way to tell me and Benjamin apart. I guess it's kinda lucky that I was jumpin' on the bed and fell on the bedpost."

Amy's nose scrunched. "I don't know that I'd call it lucky."

Benjamin looked up from where he was fussing with a stubborn button. "He had to get three stitches. With a needle and everything."

"I'll bet that hurt," Amy said.

"Nah. Not even a little bit." But Jeremiah's chest puffed as he scoffed at the experience. Then he added, "The doctor numbed my chin."

His brother's eyes widened. "With a needle."

"Mom still teases me about it," Jeremiah added, "because I started snorin' while the doctor was puttin' in the stitches."

"When did all this happen?" Amy asked.

"A couple of years ago," he told her. "When I was really little."

She wrestled with the grin that tugged at one corner of her mouth. One thing she'd learned in the past five days of caring for the boys was that there was nothing quite like experiencing life through the eyes of a child.

"Ah, so it happened when you were a petit garçon." She did her best to implement a perfect accent when she spoke the last two words.

"What's that?" Jeremiah asked.

Amy chuckled. "That means 'little boy' in French."

"You can talk in French?" Benjamin looked to be in awe.

"Don't be too impressed." She grinned. "I'm not very good. When I was a little girl I had teachers who were trained in France." She didn't think the boys would understand about the Oblate Sisters and the life of spiritual devotion they chose, so she just stuck to a simple explanation. "They introduced me to the language. All the students had to take French lessons, from the youngest to the oldest. I've tried to keep up with it by listening to audio tapes."

"Cool," Jeremiah said.

"Can you teach us some?" Benjamin's gaze lit with curiosity.

"Sure I can," she told them. "If you really want to learn." She ruffled Jeremiah's head of dark hair. "I think the luckiest thing about your ordeal with the bedpost is that your scar is so small. I have to squint to see it. But it is good to know I have a way of knowing which one of you I'm talking to.'' She smiled as she tapped the boy on the tip of his chin with the pad of her index finger, and then she reached to help Benjamin fasten his button.

Life had fallen into a comfortable routine very quickly, and that had surprised Amy. She'd wake early and get herself ready for the day. She'd help the boys dress, feed them breakfast and then they would plan the day's activities.

One day she'd taken them to Glory's public library, where they had found a huge globe on which Amy had pointed out Africa and the wide expanse of the Atlantic Ocean. Then they had read some children's books about the area where the boys' parents were serving as missionaries. They had spent another day exploring the small town of Glory together, and Benjamin and Jeremiah had been more than happy to point out the pizza place, the ice cream shop and the arcade. And yesterday she'd helped the boys pull out the fishing gear. Unable to deal with the idea of worms, she'd baited the hooks with bits of ham she'd found in the fridge. But they hadn't gotten a single nibble, so the three of them had climbed on boulders at one end of the cove and watched the blue crabs shimmy sideways under the water.

Pierce had been right when he'd told her she needed to rethink her attire. The tailored skirts and dresses that had helped to bolster her confidence since her flight training simply weren't appropriate for traipsing around after the twins. To be honest, even the slacks and leather flats she'd reverted to wearing were still not fitting for this job. What she needed was sturdier, more casual clothing. Jeans and shorts, sneakers and sandals. The stuff she used to knock around in back in Kansas. However, she'd purposely yet unfortunately left those items in her dresser back home.

During her flight attendant training, it had been stressed to her over and over again that if she wanted to garner the respect due a professional, then she must be perceived as a professional. She had to dress and act the part.

One day during her training something had clicked. She'd realized that if she looked and acted assured and capable, that's what people would believe her to be—no matter what she felt inside, no matter how lacking her background. That had been the day she'd resolved to put on the armor that would protect her from her past: carefully applied makeup, hair that was styled, coordinated apparel and a cool, confident air.

She would make herself into what she was not. And no one would be the wiser. So far, her plan had worked like a charm.

However, climbing around on wet rocks wasn't easy when you didn't have a pair of rubber-soled shoes handy. Well, that was something she'd just have to deal with. Keeping her professional facade intact was more important than sore feet.

"What's for breakfast today?" Benjamin asked, pulling her out of her thoughts.

"What would you like?" She reached out and straightened the collar of his red cotton polo shirt.

"I'd like pancakes!"

"Me, too."

Amy grinned. "Then pancakes it is."

The boys cheered and raced from the room.

"Don't run," she called after them. But she'd learned that while the boys might want to listen and obey, there was something in their small bodies that urged them to attempt to fly. Everywhere they went.

Hurrying down the steps, she paused in the front hall to answer the ringing phone.

"Dad!" Her heart warmed when she heard her father's voice. "I'm just fine. Everything is going great. I'm so glad you called."

They talked for only a couple of minutes before she told him she had to get the boys fed, but she promised to call him for a nice long chat on her day off. She set the telephone receiver into its cradle and headed down the hallway.

The kitchen was empty. In fact, the whole house felt still.

Amy stood in the quiet for the length of several heartbeats. Then anxiety washed over her as her pulse thundered and the fine hair on her arms stood on end.

The bay!

She remembered how panicky she'd been seeing the boys out on the water in the boat the day she'd arrived. She rushed out onto the sunporch, scanning the yard and the shoreline. Seeing the rowboat right where it was supposed to be, she gulped in a relieved breath.

Amy went out into the sunshine and called out the boys' names. Where could they have gone so quickly?

That's when she saw that the door to the greenhouse was open.

"Oh, Lord," she murmured. She hurried across the

lawn, knowing without a doubt that the twins had intruded on their uncle's work.

Had something like this happened when she'd first arrived, she'd have been panic-stricken about how Pierce might react to being interrupted, how he might respond to her falling down on the job and losing sight of his nephews. However, she'd learned a thing or two about the doctor.

He was a bona fide workaholic, yes. But although he often lost himself in his research, he genuinely loved Benjamin and Jeremiah. Whenever he saw them, his face lit up with pleasure. That thought made her smile even now. She'd arrived in this house expecting to face a daunting intellectual who would make her feel totally self-conscious. But Pierce's tendency toward absentmindedness somehow made him… safe. It took away all reason for her to feel ill at ease. In fact, she'd started experiencing the peculiar sensation of wanting to take care of the man.

Take dinnertime, for instance. That first night they had talked in his study, he had told her that he'd like to join her and the boys for their evening meal. But Pierce apparently had become so wrapped up in his research that he'd worked straight through dinner the following two consecutive nights. So Amy had taken to making him a plate, wrapping it up so it wouldn't dry out and slipping it into a warm oven so he'd have something to eat whenever he surfaced from his study or his lab or the greenhouse.

She stepped inside the building, cognizant that the air was warmer and more humid than outside. The greenhouse was long and fairly narrow, something you might find in a botanical garden rather than on someone's personal property.

"Benjamin? Jeremiah?"

The foliage on the plants was thick and glossy and green, and the atmosphere took on a heavy feeling, rich with oxygen, as she made her way down one aisle.

"Over here," she heard one of the boys call out.

"We're helping Uncle Pierce," the other said.

"Come join us, Amy."

From the tone of Pierce's voice he didn't sound at all annoyed that the boys had invaded his space. When she reached them, she saw that the twins were standing on stools at a planting table. Both of them had dirt smeared up to their elbows. Jeremiah was tamping down soil in what looked to be a plastic seedling tray and Benjamin was accepting a palmful of tiny seeds from his uncle.

"These seeds are special, Amy," Benjamin told her. "Uncle Pierce made 'em with cross-pollimation."

"Cross-poll*ina*tion," Pierce corrected.

"And Uncle Pierce told us that seeds were first made like this," Benjamin continued, "by a man who lost his mind."

"Lost his mind? When did I say that?" Bewilderment bit into Pierce's forehead.

Benjamin said, "You said he was mental."

"Not mental." Pierce chuckled as he shook his head. "Mendel. His name was Mendel. Gregor Mendel."

"Oh." The child looked momentarily confused. "I

thought you were telling us that the guy was crazy to try to, you know…cross-pollinate plants.''

The sigh that issued from Pierce was brimming with good-humored surrender.

Jeremiah reached up and scratched his nose, smudging the bridge of it with soil. ''Amy, I betcha didn't know that there are mommy plants and daddy plants. Just like people. Uncle Pierce was telling us that when they rub on each other, they make seeds 'steada babies.''

''Yeah,'' Benjamin added without lifting his eyes from his work. ''Plant sex.''

This completely unexpected detour in the conversation stunned Amy into silence. She lifted her gaze and saw that all the color had drained from Pierce's handsome face. His lips parted in disbelief. Evidently he was having trouble finding his tongue, too.

What was so mind-blowing was not only what the twins had said, but also how they'd said it. They'd spoken as if the topic was no big deal, honestly detailing in their own words what Pierce had evidently explained to them.

The children didn't even look up from the task at hand. Benjamin had passed his brother some of the seeds and their fingers were busy carefully sprinkling them over the soil in the seedling tray.

Her eyes locked on Pierce's mortified green gaze. Heat flushed his face. He forced his jaw closed. He swallowed. Then he moistened his lips.

Finally he whispered, ''That wasn't quite how I put things. I never once mentioned the word *sex*.''

The situation struck a humorous chord in her all of a sudden, but the menacing look he gave her made it clear that he would not appreciate it if she surrendered to the laughter that bubbled in the back of her throat. So she did all she could to squelch it.

Evidently Benjamin noticed how quiet the adults had become. He lifted his chin, looked from Amy to his uncle.

"Oh, it's okay, Uncle Pierce," he said easily. "Me and Jeremiah know all about sex."

His brother nodded, adding, "Daddy doesn't know it, but our mommy watches soap operas."

The candidness expressed by the children tickled Amy's funny bone all the more. But Pierce didn't seem to find any humor in the moment. He looked downright horrified.

"All done," Benjamin announced. "Do we need to water the seeds, Uncle Pierce?"

"Yes. Go over there to the sink—" Pierce pointed the way "—and fill up the watering can."

The boys scrambled down from the stools and raced off.

"No running," Amy called out. "You'll fall and hurt yourselves."

She was in a quandary. She was trying hard not to smile, but she also felt awkwardness pressing in on them.

Then he murmured, "I'm going to have to speak to my sister about her television viewing habits."

Amy could stand it no more. Laughter gurgled forth. Her hand flew to cover her lips. But air rushed between her fingers, her cheeks stretched in a wide grin, her shoulders shuddered up and down.

"I'm sorry," she blurted, but it was hopeless. "It's just...funny."

A corner of Pierce's mouth quirked once, twice, and soon he was chuckling right along with her.

"It is pretty funny," he agreed.

"What's funny?" Jeremiah lugged the pail over, and it was so full that water sloshed over the rim.

Ignoring his nephew's question, Pierce asked one of his own. "So you've decided to sprout those seeds hydroponically, huh?"

Benjamin's whole face screwed up. "Hydro what?"

"In water," he explained.

"But we've already planted 'em in dirt," Jeremiah pointed out, confusion knitting his forehead.

"It was a joke," Pierce told him. "Here, let me help you."

He took the watering can and sprinkled the seeds.

Amy noticed how the muscles in his forearm firmed into long cords under his skin as he maneuvered the can. Like metal attracted by a magnetic current, she was helpless against the urge to move closer.

He smelled good. She didn't want to notice the luscious heated scent of him, but she was helpless against that, as well.

"Are those seeds part of that new contract work you've started?" she asked, craning her neck to see around his shoulder.

"No, those are hybrids. I have several flats in different stages of growth, so I need to vigilantly protect them from any foreign pollen."

After only a second, she gasped. "But I left the greenhouse door open."

"It's okay," he assured her. "The seedlings are across the way in the lab, where I can monitor and control everything. Soil and air temperature, humidity, nutrient intake.''

Curiosity caught her in its grasp. ''I've heard of hybrid plants. I've probably even seen them. But I've never been sure exactly what that term means.''

''Hybrid means heterogeneous in—'' He stopped suddenly, twisting to face her as he seemed to rethink his explanation. ''It means a plant or animal that's the offspring of unlike parents.

''Hybrid plants are cultivated for different reasons,'' he continued, his gaze becoming intense. ''Sometimes people want flowers with variegated leaves or petals. Or bigger blossoms. Or a hardier root system.''

''And what are you going for?'' she asked. ''In your experiments, I mean.''

''I'm cultivating flowers for new scents. A perfumery in France has agreed to finance the experiments, and if I can cultivate something usable, they'll get a portion of the seeds. I'll get the right to patent the scent and publish the work in scientific journals.''

''So you're going to grow flowers that smell different from any other flowers in the whole wide world?'' Benjamin looked quite impressed.

''I'm trying. In fact, I've grown a small sample batch for their approval. They have those in their labs. And now I'm working on cultivating more seeds.''

''Cool.''

''Can we see your lab, Uncle Pierce?'' Jeremiah asked.

''Not today, boys.''

They groaned and complained.

Amy wondered just how amazingly intelligent a

person would have to be to take two different species of flower and create something brand-new, something that no one had ever seen—or smelled—before. There had been a passion sparkling in his gorgeous green eyes as he'd talked about his work, and she'd found that alluring.

"Some other time," he told the boys. "I've got data books scattered about in there. I'll have to clean up before you come look around. But I promise you can check everything out really soon, okay?"

Although they didn't like it, they finally acquiesced. And as children usually do, they then quickly changed the subject.

"I'm hungry," Jeremiah pronounced.

"Yeah." Benjamin piped up, "I'm ready for some pancakes."

"Both of you need to go get washed up before you do anything else," their uncle told them.

"Let's go!" They took flight down the row of plants.

"Slow down," Pierce called after them. Then he directed his gaze at Amy. "What is it?" he asked her.

"N-nothing." She was embarrassed that he'd caught her so deep in thought—about him. "I should make the boys their breakfast. I...I'm terribly sorry they barged in on you. I took a quick call from my dad."

"Is he okay?"

"Yes, yes." Her head bobbed. "He just wanted to say hi. I told him I'd call him later. I was only on the phone for a minute or two, but—" she grimaced "—Benjamin and Jeremiah were out of the house like a flash. I'll try not to let it happen again.'' She turned to leave.

''Wait.'' His fingers slid over her forearm. ''You really looked contemplative a second ago. You obviously had something on your mind. And I'd like to know what it was.''

What would it hurt to tell him? Anyone could have had the same reaction to all that he'd revealed.

''I was just overwhelmed by the very idea of it,'' she said. ''The thought of creating something original. Something that, well—'' she decided Benjamin's words had been perfect ''—no one else in the whole world has ever seen.''

''It's nothing, really.''

His tone was low. Soothing as a cool hand against a warm brow. Her skin tingled as if he were actually stroking her face with his fingertips.

''Just a little plant sex.''

Pierce's green eyes glittered mischievously...and Amy burst out laughing.

Later that night Amy was unable to sleep, so she crept down the darkened hallway and into the bathroom. The origin of this edginess jittering through her was unknown, but there was nothing that a good long soak couldn't cure.

She'd already taken her hair down and had given it a good brush when she'd gotten ready for bed. Twisting the length of it, she pinned it up so it wouldn't get wet. Then she turned on the taps and adjusted the water temperature.

Untying the sash of her robe, she shrugged it off and let it fall in a heap to the floor. She tugged her nightgown over her head, pulled off her panties and then stepped into the bathtub.

She'd had an exhausting day. Maybe her problem was that she was simply overtired.

When she'd suggested to the boys that they make cupcakes, Benjamin and Jeremiah had eagerly gathered the eggs, the flour, the sugar and the cooking utensils. By the time they had finished the job, though, the kitchen had been a mess. She'd packed up some sandwiches, fruit, juice and a few cupcakes, and they had gone outside in the backyard for a picnic. Then they had spent the entire afternoon running among the trees and shrubs.

But time and again, Amy had found her gaze drifting to the greenhouse. Pierce had intruded on her thoughts every few moments, and her mind had been bombarded by all sorts of questions.

How had he earned the money to build such an impressive business setup? Did a plant scientist command that kind of income? There were acres and acres of ground here on the shores of the Delaware Bay. He had a small laboratory and a huge greenhouse in which he performed his experiments on plants. And his house was beautiful. A dream home, really. His private library was stocked with all sorts of books on botany. Shelves of them, floor to ceiling.

She closed her eyes, and immediately her mind was filled with the image of his sparkling green gaze. His features had grown animated when he'd talked to his nephews—to her—about his work. He was an intense man. An intelligent man. An incredibly handsome man.

He was tall and sturdy. Built like a well-honed athlete rather than a scientist.

That thought made her smile. What kind of body would a scientist-type have? She'd never really thought about it before. But she could easily imagine that a man who was so focused on research and experiments would be stuck in the library with his nose in a book, or in the lab bent over a microscope. But Pierce looked tanned and healthy. His muscles were toned—she'd seen that for herself today as he'd lifted the watering pail.

The faucet gurgled, the warm water that filled the tub caressing her skin as it rose higher and higher. It was so easy to envision the tickle of the water replaced by Pierce's touch, his fingertips stroking her flesh ever so lightly.

Yes, he was the most handsome man she'd ever met in her life. However, she'd been surprised this morning to discover just how fascinated she was by his intellect. Normally she tended to avoid people who held titles and diplomas, people who had letters of educational distinction after their names. But when Pierce had talked about his work, she'd felt…drawn to him.

She sighed and thought of his perfect mouth, wondered what it would feel like on hers, imagined what his lips would taste like. Suddenly in her mind's eye she saw his tapered fingers, and then with very little conjuring she could almost feel his touch on her skin. His flesh was hot against her own. She envisioned placing her hand on the back of his, guiding his palm over her taut stomach, up toward her breasts until his fingertips were snuggled between them.

Again she sighed, and her back arched languidly in the heated bathwater.

Then her eyes opened wide. She blinked, and then she sat up so quickly that water sloshed onto the floor. What was she doing? Had she lost her mind?

Avoiding these kinds of situations, these kinds of feelings, had been her number one priority for years. Wasn't it sensual urges just like the ones floating around in her head that had caused her friends to ruin their lives?

Amy had watched as, one by one, her friends had fallen in love, gotten married and then gotten themselves pregnant. Sometimes not even in that order. But regardless of *how* they had gone about falling into the trap, they still had fallen. Right into the deadly snare.

Stuck for life in that small Podunk town. Never going anywhere. Never experiencing anything. That was the future her friends back in Lebo had relegated themselves to.

Oh, she'd allowed herself to date back home. She'd go out with a guy a time or two, maybe even three if he didn't appeal to her too much. But once she got that bug…the moment she felt that first inkling that the relationship might develop into something beyond cordial, she'd nip it right in the bud.

She'd broken a heart or two back in Kansas. But that couldn't be helped. She had a plan for her life.

The loofah sponge she snatched up felt rough against her fingers. She squirted some bath gel onto its surface and began scrubbing her skin in tiny circular motions.

A slight panic began to roil in her as Pierce's face

loomed in her brain, his green eyes tempting her, his perfect mouth enticing her.

She wasn't going to ruin her plan, darn it! She'd just finished training as a flight attendant. She'd succeeded in getting out. She'd escaped the trap. She had a whole world to see. A slew of experiences to…well, to experience.

She wasn't going to let a little sexual urge get in her way.

Amy, a small voice in the back of her mind intoned, *just because you're attracted to Pierce Kincaid doesn't mean you have to act on it. Control. That's all it takes. You can certainly ignore this temptation for the couple of months it will take for Jeremiah and Benjamin's parents to return.*

Pierce would never be interested in her, anyway— of that she was sure. Not unless she began to sprout stems and leaves and big, fat flower blossoms.

"And there's little chance of that happening," she murmured to herself.

She inhaled deeply, let the air leave her in a rush. She relaxed. Control slowly returned.

Perception really was everything.

If she chose to perceive this situation as safe and nonthreatening to her life plan, then that's exactly what it would become.

And heaven knew she didn't need to worry about Pierce noticing her as anything more than the temporary nanny who was caring for his nephews. No, she had no worries there.

Pierce lay in the dark, staring at the ceiling. Ten minutes ago, he'd heard the water running in the bathroom down the hall. Evidently unable to sleep, Amy must have decided to have a bath.

At first he'd fought his imagination. He'd tried to ignore the image his brain conjured up of her slipping out of her nightgown, shimmying out of her lacy undergarments. But the more he attempted to disregard the inappropriate thoughts, the stronger and more persistent they seemed to become.

He ''saw'' her lift one milky foot, then the other, to step into the tub, and then his mind's eye watched as she eased her delectable body down into the water. Sweat broke out on his brow and his pulse skittered. Pierce kicked the sheet aside in an attempt to cool the fever rushing through him.

This was wrong. He'd decided a long time ago that his work was more important than anything else. *Any*thing else.

He didn't want to think of Amy in a sexual manner—no, these thoughts were softer, fuzzier, and could only be described as a *sensual* manner. But whatever manner they were, he didn't want this. Not when he knew nothing could ever come of it. Nothing lasting, that was.

He rolled over onto his side, punched the pillow, shifted to a comfortable position and willed sleep to come. And when that didn't work, he prayed for release from this sweet agony.

However, all too soon he found himself on his back once again, staring at the ceiling...dreaming of the naked nanny.

Chapter Three

Sitting down at his work table in the lab, Pierce picked up a pen with the intention of recording the seedling growth measurement in his data notebook. But the exact number of centimeters dissolved from his mind as if it had been spun candy on his tongue.

But he'd just measured the darned things.

He tossed down the pen and went back to the seedling tray with his calibrated ruler in hand.

As he leaned over the tray of delicate sprouts, eyes the color of toasted cinnamon loomed in his mind. He straightened, his head tilting slightly to the side unwittingly as he pondered the color of Amy's hair. It was light brown, of course, but that just seemed too ordinary a description and left him searching for a truer one. There were blond strands that brought out a…a hue that was almost…butterscotch.

He smiled. That was it. Butterscotch.

Pierce went back to the worktable, set down the

ruler, picked up his pen—and promptly discovered that he hadn't even taken the seedling's measurements.

Dropping the pen, he scrubbed at his face with both hands. Work had gone slowly all day. He had been preoccupied.

With Amy.

Last night his imagination had been stirred to a near frenzy as he'd envisioned her in the tub, the heated water lapping against her creamy flesh—

This was ridiculous. He heaved a sigh and snapped off the light on the table. It was time for him to get away from the lab for a while. He looked at his wristwatch and saw that once again he'd missed dinner with the boys.

He placed the tray of seedlings into the containment chamber, closed the data books and replaced them on the shelves. Tomorrow was another day. Maybe it would be one in which his head was clearer, his mind more focused.

The sky was dark when he locked the door of his lab and made his way across the lawn. He entered through the French doors at the back of the house and locked up behind himself. He could hear the muffled sounds of the television.

"Hi, boys," he called when he reached the family room. Then he directed his eyes to Amy. "Hi."

A smile invaded his face, his entire being.

And when she smiled back, he actually went buoyant inside.

"Hungry?" she asked. "You worked through dinner." One corner of her mouth quirked. "Again."

His nerve endings trilled and heat curled low in his

gut at the sexy sight she made sitting there grinning at him...showing concern for him.

"I am, actually. Hungry, I mean."

For food? a tiny voice whispered from the back of his head. *Or for Amy?*

In a flash, all the fervor pulsing through him turned dour. He'd already told himself that he shouldn't be toying with this attraction he felt for the nanny, hadn't he? He wasn't fit relationship material. He knew that. Had figured it out long ago.

"Come on, then," she told him, pushing herself up from the sofa. "I'll fix you something." She looked at the twins. "I'll bring you back some popcorn and juice—would you like that?"

Both boys gave her an enthusiastic answer.

Softly she said, "Let's go."

Why hadn't he spoken up? Why hadn't he told her he was perfectly capable of finding himself something to eat?

Because he wanted to follow her gently swaying fanny into the kitchen, that's why.

Amy placed a bag of popcorn into the microwave oven and pushed the buttons to turn it on. As she pulled down glasses for the boys' drinks, she told Pierce, "Benjamin and Jeremiah asked for soup and grilled cheese sandwiches for dinner tonight. There's soup left. And it will only take me a minute or two to grill a sandwich for you. Will that be okay?"

"That will be fine."

She poured juice into the glasses and set a bowl on the counter for the popcorn. Then she went to the fridge and took out the container of leftover soup, the cheese and the butter. She pulled two slices of sour-dough bread from the package.

"How did you know?" he asked, unable to hide the pleasure that shot through him.

Her features registered bewilderment. "How did I know what?"

"That sourdough is my favorite type of bread."

"I didn't. This was the bread in the bread box."

Embarrassment had him going quiet. The momentary burst of delight had him feeling silly.

"I can do this. You're not here to cater to my needs."

"I don't mind," she said in a rush. "Really. Please."

Something in her face made him pause.

Then she sighed. "I could use a little adult conversation. Being with the twins is great, don't get me wrong. But it would be nice to talk for five whole minutes without being asked 'why this' or 'why that,' if you know what I mean."

The sweet sound of her chuckle seemed to smooth over all the rough edges his emotions had suddenly developed. He smiled.

"I do know what you mean," he said.

She'd slathered butter on the bread and assembled the sandwich in the skillet when the microwave beeped at the end of its cooking cycle. She quickly emptied the popcorn into the bowl, and then placed the bowl and the glasses of juice on a tray.

"Watch the sandwich," she told him. "I'll be right back."

Okay. Now that he was alone, he could take the

time to clear his head. He could spend a few seconds rationalizing with himself.

What he needed to do was hightail it out of here. Just make some excuse to take his dinner into the study.

But that would be rude. The woman was living in his home. She was watching his nephews. He had to interact with her a little, didn't he?

And besides that, she'd just said she was keen on some dialogue that was a little more sophisticated than could be provided by his six-year-old nephews.

The instant Pierce closed his eyes the image of her perfectly styled butterscotch hair floated into his brain, and he envisioned removing the clips or whatever held it in place, running his fingers through the soft locks.

"Oh, no!"

Her yelp had his eyes snapping open.

Smoke billowed from the pan on the burner. He swore under his breath and automatically reached for the handle.

"Wait!" she shouted. "Use a pot holder!"

He snatched up the pot holder and took the skillet off the burner.

"Your sandwich is ruined."

She was next to him as she made the verdict. The lemony sunshine scent of her mingled with the smell of smoke and charred bread.

"And it's all my fault. I—I should have been watching."

"Well, there's no harm done really." She opened the bread box and reached for two more slices. "I can start over again." Amy grinned, cutting her brown eyes up at him. "Were you thinking about your work?"

Oh, if that had only been the case, he thought as he dumped the burned sandwich into the garbage disposal. Then he wadded up a paper towel and swiped the pan clean.

Without waiting for an answer, she said, "You do get lost in all those thoughts churning around in your head." She laughed as she buttered the bread.

When she nodded that she was ready, he slid the skillet back onto the burner. She plopped the bread slice into it and the butter sizzled. She added cheese and then a second slice of buttered bread.

"Is your experiment going okay?"

He nodded. "Everything's going according to plan."

"Well, that's good." She ladled soup into a small saucepan and set it to heat on a back burner.

"Yes." Pierce realized he was smiling now that a full catastrophe had been avoided. "Yes, it is."

Without missing a beat, Amy said, "The boys and I have spent the past few days exploring the grounds. You've got the bay. You've got the gardens. There's even a thicket of trees. It's beautiful. Did you and your sister grow up here?"

"We did." He rested his hip on the corner of the countertop. "And it was a great place to grow up. Of course, the grounds didn't look anything like this when I was a kid. It was a piece of waterfront property filled with scrub and weeds and nothing on it but a small ranch house. My mother spent her whole life planting the gardens and making this property into what it is today."

Amy flipped the sandwich. "How about the green-house and the lab?"

"My father had those built," Pierce told her.

She set down the spatula and used a spoon to stir the soup.

"He made a small fortune with several patents he filed." Quietly he added, "He spent his whole life in those buildings out there."

A gloomy cloud began to gather as thoughts of his father swarmed around in Pierce's head. He did what he could to shove them to the back of his mind. Amy wanted upbeat conversation. Talking about his father would not fill that bill.

Focusing on memories of his mother's smiling face, her glittering eyes, Pierce inhaled deeply and crossed his arms over his chest. "My mother had my sister and me late in her life. But that didn't keep her from being a great mom. She made sure that Cyn and I had everything we needed. We were her life. And Cyn and I just about worshiped the ground Mom walked on."

He realized that talking about his mother had lifted the heaviness in his chest.

"My sister's only a year younger than I am," he went on, "so we did everything together. I can remember the year Mom taught us to swim. Cyn didn't catch on as quickly as I did." He chuckled. "What a fantastic time I had ribbing her about that, too."

Amy was quiet for a moment as she seemed pre-occupied with scooping the sandwich from the pan and putting it on a plate. Quietly she said, "But she did learn in the end, didn't she?"

The tentativeness in her tone made his head cock a fraction.

Her shoulders rounded and she busied herself with filling a bowl with soup as she finally admitted, "She's better off than me."

"You can't swim?"

She refused to look at him as she shook her head in answer.

He watched her carry his dinner to the table, and the vulnerability he sensed emanating from her overwhelmed him. Shocked him, really. It was so at odds with the confident woman he knew her to be.

"You can't swim, yet you didn't hesitate about going into the bay after the boys the day you arrived. I think that was pretty brave of you."

Keeping her eyes averted, she murmured, "Anyone would have done the same." Amy turned to face him. "There's something that's been bothering me. I'm pretty sure the boys can't swim." She moistened her lips. "I asked them about it, and they told me their mom and dad have taken them into the bay and to a community pool, but they didn't quite convince me about their swimming abilities. They've asked to go into the water when it warms up, but..."

"Well, I could teach them to swim," he said, walking over to where she stood. "I could teach you, too."

She stared at him for the length of several heartbeats. "You, um, wouldn't mind?"

"Of course not."

Then she blurted, "We could do it on my scheduled day off. On a day you expected to be with the boys. That way we wouldn't be taking you away from your work."

It was clear to him that she felt the lessons would be inconveniencing him. This was a side of her he hadn't seen before. This defenselessness made her seem softer, less self-assured…and much less intimidating to him.

Pierce felt the sudden urge to go out of his way to do something nice for her.

"Amy—" his tone took on a feathery lightness that pulled her gaze to his "—you're in no way putting me out. In fact, I think it's an important safety issue. It's dangerous for the boys to be around the water if they're unable to swim."

She continued to look ill at ease. Reaching out, he placed his hands on her forearms. The moment he made contact with her, he realized that touching her had been a mistake.

His whole body came alive. All his senses were heightened. He could actually hear the sound of her breathing. The heat of her scorched his palms. The light citrusy scent of her filled his lungs. The sight of her beautiful face loomed in his mind. The only sensation that wasn't working in that instant was that of taste.

And he was dying to savor the sweetness of her lips.

The discomfort that had her brow furrowing was all that kept him from surrendering to the urge.

In an effort to somehow take away her uneasiness, he pulled himself out of the haze of yearning long enough to assure her, "I mean it, Amy. And we don't have to do it on your day off." He attempted to chuckle, and hoped it sounded lighter to her than it did to his own ears. "It's not as if I spend every waking moment in the lab and the greenhouse."

Suddenly she seemed to calm. Something sparked in her spicy gaze.

Humor.

"Well," she quipped, "not *every* waking moment. You do spend a few shut up in your study."

He couldn't help but laugh. "Guilty as charged."

They simultaneously fell silent, each studying the other's face. The oxygen grew thick. A current hung between them, humming like the leftover vibrations in a multitude of just-stroked harp strings.

Lord above, but she was gorgeous. Her upswept hair emphasized the long length of her milky neck, not to mention her oh-so-kissable jawline. Cheekbones, nose, brow…all were fine and delicate, as if they'd been sculpted by some heaven-blessed artist.

His brain had gone foggy again, he realized. Why else would his analytical mind have become so fanciful?

My, how desperately he wanted to taste that delectable mouth of hers. Her top lip crested in a perfect bow, and the bottom one was lusciously full, tempting him to do what his brain knew he should not.

The seconds seemed to throb by. Or was that his pulse?

As if by its own volition, his hand rose and he ran the backs of his fingers lightly along her cheek.

Just as he'd thought—her skin was like velvet.

His touch affected her. He saw something ignite in her eyes. First her gaze lit with what was more than a smidgen of surprise. Then attraction blazed to life.

The emotion was as clear as sunlight on a cloudless day.

Seeing that what she had provoked in him was right in line with what his touch provoked in her, he wanted to smile. However, he didn't. He simply couldn't. He was as taken aback by the intensity enveloping them as she obviously was. The concentrated power that swirled and danced and frolicked all around the two of them shocked him. Stunned him, really.

A cloud shadowed her dark eyes, and she stepped away from him. Stepped away from his outstretched hand.

She averted her gaze, and her voice was husky as she murmured, "I—I can't do this."

Sanity returned so quickly that he nearly jerked with the jolt of it. "I'm sorry, Amy," he rushed to say. "I didn't know you had a boyfriend...that you were...spoken for."

She looked at him, shaking her head nervously. "Oh, I'm not. I don't. It's not that at all."

Her agitation had her moistening her delectable lips, the sight nearly sinking Pierce up to the knees in that quicksand of craving once again. Nearly. But acute curiosity over what she said kept his head clear.

"It's not that I can't—" Again her tongue darted across her lips, nerve impulses kicking in and forcing her to swallow. "It's that...I don't want to."

"Do you *have* to go off without us today?" Benjamin voiced the question in a plaintive whine.

Ruffling his hair, Amy grinned. "It's my day off. Everyone deserves a day off, don't they? I'm going to go to the store. I'll look for a new dress. Maybe a pair of nice pants. Some high heels. Stockings. Who knows what I might end up with? You wouldn't be interested in shopping with me.''

The boy's whole face lit like a hundred-watt bulb. ''I would if you were shopping at a toy store.''

Having offered to feed the twins and get them ready for the day, Amy now waited on the patio for Pierce, who was showering. She was actually looking forward to exploring some of the women's apparel shops in town.

She laughed at Benjamin's comment. ''Well, there's not a single toy store on my list of places to visit today.''

''Oh.'' True disappointment clouded his gaze.

''But just think,'' she quickly added in an attempt to lift his spirits, ''you and your brother get to spend the whole day with your uncle Pierce. That should be fun.''

He agreed with her, then ran out into the yard to join Jeremiah.

Amy flipped through a beauty magazine, studying the pictures of the gorgeous models and the how-to articles she had taken to turning to for makeup and wardrobe suggestions.

She didn't really need this day away from the twins. Yes, the boys had required every ounce of her attention this past week, but she'd enjoyed it more than she'd expected to. Six-year-old boys were prone to say just about anything that was on their minds, and Amy had found herself laughing at their antics more often than not. Taking the boys with her for a day of shopping wouldn't have been something she'd have objected to. But Pierce would have opposed it. He'd told her she was due a day off, and he was adamant that she take it.

A model smiled at her from a full-page advertisement for a new summery shade of lip gloss that caught Amy's eye. The woman's hair and skin color were a close match to Amy's, and she made a mental note to purchase a tube of the shimmery lipstick.

When she'd been accepted into the flight attendant training course, she'd been ecstatic. All she'd ever wanted to do was see the world. During her weeks of instruction sessions, she'd learned all about the different models of airplanes, how to treat her customers and what to do during an emergency. She'd also learned how important demeanor was, how essential outside appearance was when the intent was to look professional. She'd learned that the body spoke an entire language all its own.

A woman whose spine was straight, whose shoulders were square, whose gaze was level and steady not only appeared self-assured, competent and worthy of respect, she was most often treated that way, as well. The attitude one projected was...well, it meant the difference between success and failure. The difference between being taken seriously and being dismissed out of hand.

Having been raised by her father, Amy had grown up working hard alongside him to make their small motel business a success. She'd never had the opportunity to play dress-up like other young girls. When your life consisted of changing bed linens, scrubbing toilets and bathtubs, dusting and vacuuming, keeping the accounts, greeting customers and seeing to their needs, looking attractive never really entered your head. There was no need for makeup or pretty clothes or smart hairstyles when there were what seemed a thousand chores needing to be done each and every day.

But Amy's training instructor had changed her thinking completely. A dab or two of mascara, a swipe of eyeliner, a flick of blush, a smear of lipstick—those things got a girl noticed. She'd never forget when this revelation had struck her full force.

The other young women in the training class had seemed to understand that liquid foundation smoothed the color of a woman's skin, that it needed to be set with loose facial power and that contour powder could be used to give the illusion of a narrow nose or higher cheekbones. Amy, on the other hand, had been ignorant of all these things.

Oh, there were plenty of things she did know. But knowing how to keep credit card and cash receipts organized and tallied for the IRS, or how to remove all sorts of stains from white cotton sheets and carpeting wasn't the kind of knowledge that an airline flight attendant needed.

So Mary Beth, her instructor, had taken her aside for some private sessions in the application of makeup, hairstyling and fashion. Those lessons had changed Amy's life…changed her whole outlook on herself.

She had been astounded by what a little tweezing and shaping, what a little tinted powder and gloss could do for a woman's face. Amy had actually felt pretty as she'd stared into the mirror.

She smiled even now as she thought about the reaction of an extraordinarily handsome man she'd met after one particular session. Mary Beth's brother had come to the center to visit his sister, and as Amy had left the room…he'd stared. He'd called after her. And then he had thrilled the daylights out of her by asking her out for coffee.

Of course, Amy had declined the invitation. Going out with anyone would have been counterproductive when she was on the brink of having everything she'd ever wanted—travel and excitement, some real life experiences! But that moment had forever changed Amy's opinion of who she was. Or rather, how she wanted to project herself.

She didn't have to be a homely nobody barely worth noticing. She might be uneducated, in the formal sense of the word. She might even be downright unrefined. But she could make herself look just as sophisticated as any other young woman walking down the street of Lebo, Kansas, or Glory, Delaware, or Paris, France, for that matter.

Pierce had noticed.

Boy, had he ever.

Amy had felt attracted to Pierce from the moment she'd first laid eyes on him. The man was gorgeous, with his thick black hair and those dreamy green eyes. She'd have had to be dead not to be stirred by his smile.

However, she'd never imagined that attraction might be reciprocated. She'd been so sure that controlling her own feelings was all that she needed to do.

Apparently she'd been wrong.

When she and Pierce had been standing in the

kitchen the night before last, something amazingly potent had wrapped itself around the two of them.

She hadn't really noticed it at first. From their conversation, she'd realized that he was devoted to his mother. His affection for her had shone in his gaze when he'd spoken of her. But when Pierce had mentioned his father, Amy had become acutely aware of some darker emotion. Almost a bitterness. He had quickly moved on to other topics, but Amy couldn't deny she'd been curious about what might have caused friction between Pierce and his father.

Soon, though, Amy had become cognizant of a humming energy in the air. It had taken a moment or two, but she'd identified the electricity as allure. Never in her wildest imaginings had she thought that Pierce might be in tune with the current that zipped and twanged between them. Yet he had.

His green eyes had darkened with obvious acknowledgment. His entire countenance had gone intense, almost pensive, as silence had struck them both.

When he'd reached out and touched her face, she'd thought she was going to faint dead away. Her mind had turned into an empty void. Words and thoughts had completely failed her. But her heart had revved alarmingly and her body had heated…like the engine of some fancy race car.

Luckily, reason had cleared the fog in her brain and she'd been able to calmly tell him the truth. She was not interested in exploring the passion that thickened the air.

"Amy?"

She started, realizing from the boy's tone that Jeremiah must have spoken her name more than once in order to capture her attention.

"You okay?" he asked.

Amy nodded.

"Whatcha doin'?"

Unwilling to admit that she was daydreaming about the child's uncle, she swiftly came up with a story. "I'm just looking at the pretty ladies in my magazine here."

The boy came closer and stared down at the model with the summery-tinted lips.

"You're way prettier than she is."

Amy's heart warmed. "What a nice thing for you to say."

"This is for you," he said. He held out a yellow dandelion.

She accepted the flower with a smile of thanks. "It's lovely. You're such a sweetheart."

"I'm going to miss you today."

"I'm going to miss you, too."

Benjamin called his brother to come look at a small hill of ants, and Jeremiah raced away. She watched the twins, realizing all over again that she'd had a great deal of fun with them this past week.

Amy's gaze wandered to the magazine that lay in her lap.

You're way prettier than she is.

Jeremiah's words floated through her mind. Amy wasn't stupid enough to take the child's biased opinion as fact. But his innocent statement did start her thinking.

The very things she'd been clinging to in order to come off looking confident and competent—her physical appearance, her veneer of poise, her attitude of self-assurance—were quickly becoming a precious bane. She enjoyed wearing the persona, no matter how fake it might be. Her mask made her feel good about herself. However, the very thing she'd decided she needed in order to command respect was now leading her straight into trouble.

She didn't want Pierce to be attracted to her.

No matter how much of an enticement he was for her, she knew she could control her own emotions. All her hopes and dreams hinged on her doing just that. But she seriously doubted she could control a man like Pierce.

The magnetism that had plucked at them in the kitchen the other night could really turn into quite a problem. She didn't want to get involved in any kind of relationship that might become messy or entangling. She had too many plans to let something like that happen.

Besides that, this front she'd been presenting wasn't the real her. It was merely a guise taught to her as a way of looking professional.

Amy looked off across the bay, the blue water calming her anxious spirit.

Maybe what she needed to do was forgo the pretty part of the persona she'd created in order to become more noticeable. Maybe what she should do was slip back into that plain, unadorned Amy. Pierce wouldn't find *her* the least bit attractive.

She wasn't willing to let go of her new attitude, though. She liked looking and feeling confident. However, she *was* willing to brush her hair into a plainer style, scrub her face free of blush, foundation and eye shadow. No way would Pierce find her the lease bit alluring then.

The urge to chuckle rose in her throat. Most women hankered after a transformation that would make them more beautiful. She certainly had. But here she was contemplating a reverse makeover, an alteration meant to make her less appealing to the opposite sex—less appealing to Pierce.

"What has you grinning this morning?"

Amy looked up to see that Pierce had stepped out into the sunshine. The very sight of him in his white polo shirt and olive shorts made her feel things she knew she shouldn't. She did what she could to squelch the inappropriate impulses.

"Oh, nothing, really," she intoned as lightly as she could. "Just thinking about what I'm going to do today."

His green eyes glistened. She'd have liked to think it was just the morning sunlight that caused the glitter, but she highly suspected it was interest. In her.

He came close enough so that she could smell his cologne. His face was just-shaved smooth. Why did he have to be so darned handsome?

"I know," he said, "that I stressed how important I feel it is for you to get away from the boys on your day off, but…"

Amy's heart tripped a beat as she wondered what he had on his mind.

"I thought the four of us could do something special—" he paused long enough to moisten his lips "—together."

The suggestion surprised her. She stood up so quickly that the fashion magazine slipped from her lap and fell to the patio. She reached down and scooped it up, held it to her chest as if it were some sort of shield.

"I can't," she blurted. "I—I planned to go shopping."

Pierce looked as disappointed as young Benjamin had just a moment or two ago when he discovered he wouldn't be going along with her today.

"I—I'm sorry…" she began.

"No," he rushed to say. "That's quite all right. It's your day off. You should do whatever you like with it."

"Thanks." She edged toward the door of the house. "I'll be back around dinnertime." Amy called a quick goodbye to the twins.

She did have some shopping to do, she suddenly decided. But she wouldn't be buying any shimmering lip gloss or tailored trousers. The items she needed wouldn't be found in any exclusive women's boutiques, either. A run-of-the-mill department store would have everything she required, she was certain.

Chapter Four

The waning afternoon had turned stifling and muggy. Pierce had suggested a dip in the bay, and the sweaty boys happily agreed.

Every so often he'd remember how surprised he'd been when he'd so unexpectedly blurted out the suggestion to Amy that the four of them do something special together. After having spent the entire week in the company of the twins, Amy needed some time away from them. He'd known that. Had even stressed that opinion to her. But then he'd gone out onto the deck this morning and had invited her to spend the day with them.

He'd been amazed at his own actions.

Luckily Amy had reined in his rashness by announcing she had plans.

This day had turned out to be just great. He'd played ball in the yard with the boys for most of the morning. They'd had peanut-butter-and-jelly sandwiches for lunch. He'd shown them all around his lab. He grinned as he remembered how unimpressed they'd been with the seedlings that were taking up so much of his time. And now the three of them were splashing around in the blue-green water.

Amy's observation that Benjamin and Jeremiah couldn't swim had worried Pierce. The unseasonably warm weather presented a great opportunity to get his nephews into the cool bay to judge how much swimming skill they did or didn't possess.

Pierce quickly discerned that Amy had been correct. Both children were fearful of even putting their faces into the water, and neither was comfortable with venturing farther than knee-deep into the bay.

After an hour of clowning around and playing keep-away with a spongy rubber ball, Pierce asked the boys if they'd like to learn to swim.

Jeremiah, the more adventuresome of the two, replied that he really wanted to learn. Benjamin, on the other hand, grew quiet as a fearful shadow clouded his dark eyes.

Turning to his brother, Jeremiah said, "It's okay, Benjamin. Don't be afraid."

Benjamin's chin jutted forward with obvious affront. "I'm not ascared of anything."

"That's good." Pierce kept his tone calm in order to keep the conversation from flaring into an argument. "But you both should know that you can't learn to swim in one lesson. First you need some basics. You need to get used to getting your faces wet. You need to practice holding your breath and going under the water. You'll need to become more comfortable in the water."

The lessons went much more smoothly, he learned, when he turned each task into a game. They blew bubbles and ended up laughing at each other. They remained close to shore and took turns sitting on the sandy bottom so that the water came up over their shoulders. Finally he got them comfortable enough to dunk under the water. They both came up sputtering, but gleeful and proud that they had completed the challenge.

Pierce showed them the "dead man's float," the gory name alone igniting an overwhelming urge in both boys to try floating facedown in the water as if they had "croaked," as the twins described it. However, it took the twins quite a while to trust the fact that they could float on their backs almost as easily as they could float on their faces.

With one hand planted firmly between Benjamin's shoulder blades, Pierce coaxed the child to try lifting his feet from the bottom one more time.

"I'll sink," the boy said.

Hearing the trepidation in Benjamin's voice, Pierce promised, "I won't let that happen. Trust me."

His nephew's gaze locked on his, and Pierce felt Benjamin's body relax. His toes peeked above the surface of the water.

"It's okay," Pierce assured him. "I've got you." When it seemed that the child was ready, he asked, "You want to try it on your own?"

"Yeah." Benjamin's answer was a mere whisper.

Pierce eased his hand from his nephew's back, but remained right by his side. Then he lifted both hands above the surface so that his nephew could see them. Benjamin's mouth broke into a grin.

"I'm doing it. I'm floating."

The clapping and cheering coming from shore drew the eyes of everyone.

"Woo-hoo!" Amy jumped up and down with glee. "You did it!"

Her shiny brown hair swung loose about her shoulders, the sunlight catching bronzed highlights. It was the first time Pierce had seen Amy's hair when it wasn't styled and sprayed to perfection. His gaze was riveted on those free-flowing tresses.

"Did you see me, Amy?" Benjamin called once he'd planted his feet on the bay bottom once again. "Did you see me floating?"

"I did. And you were doing a great job out there."

Refusing to take a back seat to his brother, Jeremiah called, "Amy, watch what I can do." He held his breath, his cheeks puffing like a blowfish, and slipped beneath the water with a small splash. Immediately he popped up, and Amy applauded for him, too.

"Way to go!"

Pierce couldn't take his eyes from her. She'd... changed.

Radically.

Gone were the upscale trousers and tailored tops he'd been so used to seeing her wear this past week. The simple white cotton T-shirt had the word *princess* printed in pink across the delectable swell of her breasts. Her shorts were made of denim. And her feet were clad in simple canvas sneakers secured with plain white laces.

Something else about her was different, too, but even after he'd studied her for as long as it had taken her to greet and applaud the boys for their swimming efforts, he was unable to figure out exactly what it was.

The smile she offered his nephews was genuine. Dazzling, really. She was beautiful. He'd thought so before, but *now*...

His thoughts seemed to clunk in slow motion as he pondered the woman standing on the sandy bank.

Then he realized something else. She looked so darned...accessible. More so than ever before. The very opposite of the intimidating woman he'd deemed her to be upon her first arrival a week ago. The transformation was amazing.

Fresh. Fun loving. Affable. These were the words that flashed through his mind as he stared at her.

How could one day away from the boys cause such a drastic change?

Suddenly her nut-brown eyes were on him, and he watched as her smile dimmed a little. Her gaze wavered, fell, then met his again.

"Hello," she finally said. "You're having a good day with the boys."

She might not have been posing a question, but he answered as if she had.

"Yes. I am."

Her mouth quirked and widened into a smile, which then dwindled. Awkwardness seemed to throb from her in invisible waves.

"The activity you chose is perfect." She swiped the back of her neck with her fingers to make a point. Her hair flipped up and over the back of her hand. "I can't believe the day turned so hot."

He couldn't seem to find his tongue. Every thought

in his head was focused on how the sun glinted on those velvety tresses, how her dark eyes sparkled, how her shy smile shone.

She was expecting a response from him. He could tell. He felt like a complete idiot standing there waist-deep in the bay.

Luckily Jeremiah chose that moment to pipe up. ''Why don't you come in for a swim, Amy? Me and Benjamin can show you some more stuff that Uncle Pierce taught us today.''

Benjamin concurred with a gleeful yelp, and he smacked his splayed palms against the water's surface.

''Oh, I don't know.'' Reluctance had her looking toward the horizon.

Refusing to be put off, Jeremiah encouraged her by chanting her name. Benjamin swiftly joined in.

''A-my! A-my! A-my!''

Laughter bubbled from her, lighting her eyes, her entire face. Pierce hadn't thought he could become more mesmerized, but...

''Okay! Okay!'' she told them. ''Lucky for you guys I bought a swimsuit today. I'll be right back.''

The boys bellowed at what they saw as a great coup. All Pierce could do as he watched Amy race toward the house was feel the pounding of his heart, the rushing of his blood as it whooshed through his head.

The heat that flooded through him had nothing whatsoever to do with the blazing sun in the cloudless sky. It had everything to do with testosterone.

He wanted Amy. Even though he knew he shouldn't.

The statement she'd made last night when they'd been alone in the kitchen had intrigued him no end. The moment had turned intense, thick with attraction. She'd felt it just as blatantly as he had.

When he'd reached out to touch her, she'd pulled away from him. Her reluctance had led him to believe she had a boyfriend waiting for her back in her home-town. When he'd voiced the thought, she'd quickly set him straight.

It's not that I can't. It's that I don't want to.

She'd implied that she was free of romantic entan-glements. However, she couldn't have been clearer about the fact that she wasn't interested in any, either.

He hadn't been able to keep himself from wonder-ing why.

She was beautiful. Young. Smart. She could have the pick of the crop when it came to men. So…why wouldn't she want that? What was it that had made her turn her back on relationships?

He'd tossed and turned into the morning hours pon-dering these questions.

"Uncle Pierce!"

Swiveling his head to look at Benjamin, Pierce re-acted to the blur speeding toward him. "Whoa!" In-stinct kicked in and he was able to dodge the sopping, spongy ball that his nephew hurled at his chest. "You're in for it now," he called, trudging through the water to retrieve the ball, and tossed it at Benja-min.

Jeremiah joined in the game, and they spent some time horsing around and generally having a good time.

Pierce couldn't help but notice that both his nephews were happy children. Cynthia and John were doing a good job of raising the boys. Benjamin and Jeremiah were stable. They were well-adjusted. They were secure in the knowledge that they were loved.

Those things were clearly evident. In their easy laughter. In their candid questions. In their unguarded gazes.

As a child, Pierce knew, he'd been the direct opposite of Jeremiah and Benjamin.

Oh, he realized that his mother had done all she could to give him and Cynthia a normal childhood. She'd gone out of her way to play the role of both mother and father.

It was obvious that his sister had learned good parenting skills from their mother. The proof was right in front of him, in the happy faces of his nephews.

Pierce loved his mother for all she'd done, for all she'd attempted to provide for him. However, all the love she'd poured on him hadn't kept him from spending his entire childhood—and his young adulthood, too—feeling as if there was a hole in his heart. As though he were being trailed by a gray cloud of self-consciousness. As though there was something wrong with him, and that no matter how hard he tried, he was unworthy of notice.

Pierce had spent years longing for—striving for—the attention of someone who was…unavailable. To him. To his sister. To his mother.

That experience had affected him greatly. It had made him realize what he was. And what he wasn't. It had forced him to make some hard-line decisions about what directions his life would—

"Catch this one, Uncle Pierce!"

There was a blatant challenge in Jeremiah's tone as he reared back and flung the ball over Pierce's head. The ball sailed up into the air and out several yards to plop into the bay, where it bobbed on the water's surface.

"Now look what you've done," Benjamin complained. "Looks like the game's over. We'll never reach that ball now."

"It's okay, Benjamin," Pierce told the boy. "I'll get it."

"B-but the water's too deep."

He offered the boy a small, indulgent smile. "When you learn to swim," he said quietly, "you'll be able to go out into water that's over your head, too. And you won't have to be afraid." He dived toward deeper water, kicking his feet and pumping his arms.

Once he reached the ball, he snatched it up and twisted around, treading water, with the intention of calling to Benjamin and tossing the ball to him. But the sight of Amy striding toward the water's edge wearing a revealing bathing suit made his brain go haywire.

She was like a big swallow of cool water to his parched senses. Heat sparked deep within him, curling and spiraling low in his gut.

What was it about this young woman that provoked such an overwhelming reaction in him each and every time she was near?

"Throw the ball to Amy, Uncle Pierce!"

The idea Jeremiah planted in his head had him grinning wickedly. "Here!" he called out to her. "Catch!"

He tossed the ball, and Amy's features registered surprise. The ball landed in her hands, water splattering down her arms and across her taut stomach. She gasped, evidently just discovering that the ball was spongy and sopping.

Fire sparked in her brown gaze. "You rat!"

Momentarily, Pierce thought she just might be angry. But then he saw she was laughing and kicking off her canvas sneakers.

"I'll get you," she threatened, slogging into the bay knee-deep, where she pushed the ball beneath the water to fill it. Then she flung it directly at his head.

He howled as he easily made a catch; however, he wasn't able to keep water from spraying him in the face. He sputtered. The boys cheered.

"That sure sucks for you, Uncle Pierce!"

"Benjamin!" Amy admonished.

"Well," Jeremiah added with an ornery snicker, "it does suck for him that you splashed him so good."

"Boys!" There was caution in Pierce's tone. "I don't want you using that word again. It isn't nice. And if I hear it one more time, you'll be spending the rest of the day in your room."

Both children muttered apologies and promises to be good.

They were eager to show Amy, all over again, all they had learned. And they even surprised themselves when they began to paddle, doggy-style, through the water.

"We're swimmin'!" Benjamin shouted, catching his brother's eye. "Look at us!"

Amy looked over at Pierce. "It's a start," she said.

"They'll be swimming around here like little minnows before too long." He held her gaze for a moment. "You will be, too. If you still want me to teach you to swim, that is."

"Oh, I do," she told him. "It's not safe for the boys to be in the water without an adult who can at least come to their rescue if the need arises."

Inadvertently his gaze dipped to her cleavage…to where the stretchy bathing-suit fabric caused her breasts to swell into milky mounds. He was grateful that her attention was focused on the boys' antics.

He was actually embarrassed by his lack of self-control when it came to his physical reaction to Amy. Never before had a woman affected him so. The situation confused him.

"Uncle Pierce, I'm thirsty."

Pierce's gaze swung to the shoreline, where both boys were standing.

"Me, too," Benjamin added.

Before he could respond, Amy said, "I brought a pitcher of lemonade out when I came."

"Can we have some?"

Amy chuckled, the light, breezy sound of it making Pierce smile.

"Of course you can," she told them. "I set the pitcher and cups on the table on the deck." She turned to him. "Would you like something to drink?"

"I'm fine," he said.

The boys ran across the yard toward the house. Although his nephews were still within sight, Pierce felt as if he and Amy were pretty much alone. A sudden case of nerves fell over him.

"Well—" His voice came out rusty, like the croaking of a frog, and he paused for a quick clearing of his throat. "Would you like to have your first lesson right now?"

The edginess that had infected him must have been contagious. Amy's head bobbed, her hair swinging to brush her shoulders. Her intriguing brown gaze turned aside momentarily. Finally her eyes rose to his as she answered with a tiny nod.

The timidity she exhibited did something strange to the air surrounding him. It became hard to inhale, and even though he was standing waist-deep in the bay, he felt flushed, overheated.

As he stared at her, he realized that her face was scrubbed free of every trace of makeup. Since her arrival, he'd only seen her wearing eye shadow and lipstick and whatever else women used to enhance their beauty.

The fact Pierce comprehended in this instant, though, was that Amy didn't need any enhancing. Her skin glowed with vibrant health. Her coffee-colored eyes were perfectly framed with delicate brows, her long russet lashes creating an attractive fan.

She looked the very essence of freshness. Of vitality. And until this very instant, he'd never realized how that kind of energy enthralled him.

His heart tripped against his ribs as further insight set in. In order to teach Amy to swim, he was going to have to get close to her—*very* close to her.

"I guess we should start with the basics." He lifted his hand in a most casual gesture and was shocked to see he was trembling. Slipping his hand beneath the surface of the water, he hoped she hadn't noticed his reaction to the mere thought of touching her.

"The basics," she repeated. "Sounds good."

There was a slight tremor in her voice. He swallowed and wondered how the atmosphere could have changed so quickly, so drastically. One second they'd been cavorting playfully in the water with the boys, the next they were acting like teens who had never encountered the opposite sex.

"Um, ah," he stammered. He took a step closer to her. "Let's see how you do at floating on your back."

She hesitated.

"I realize," he hurried to say, "that being on your back will make you feel terribly vulnerable. But if you tackle that fear, you'll be all the better for it." Feeling that she was still unsure, he added, "Trust me. I promise not to let anything happen to you."

He continued to sense reluctance in her as she took the final step toward him. The faint scent of sun-warmed lemon emanated from the surface of her skin and mingled with the salty tang of the bay.

"I'll place my hand at the back of your neck," he told her. "Until you feel comfortable on your own."

Amy nodded.

His hand felt leaden as he placed one palm high on her back at the base of her neck. The other he pressed against the velvet skin of her shoulder. The force he applied was gentle, and Amy relaxed against the support he provided.

She scorched him. The pads of his fingertips and the fleshy part of his palm were flaming hot. He was surprised that steam was not rising from the surface of the water.

It was a silly notion, he knew. There was no way that the simple fact that they'd made physical contact could generate heat. The scientist in him could rationalize what was happening. The simple biology of human sexuality.

He desired this woman. He'd realized that much already.

However, Amy wasn't interested. She'd made that clear enough.

What he needed to do was eradicate this wanting from his mind. He was fairly sure he could. It was eradicating the wanting from his body that was going to be the problem.

Pierce closed his eyes, dragged in a breath and tried to obliterate every nuance of physical longing from his thoughts and transform his thinking into a void. Like the blue-green vastness of the Delaware Bay. Only then did he raise his eyelids—

And his gaze helplessly scanned the entire luscious length of her body.

Water lapped at every inch of her. It hugged her arms, embraced the ample curves of her breasts, waist and hips, cuddled her thighs, her perfect knees, those shapely calves. His eyes languished on the painted tips of her toes that peeked above the surface of the bay.

He blinked. Her eyes were closed, her breathing even as she concentrated on floating. He couldn't stop himself from feasting on the sight of her lovely face. Pierce felt like a ravenous man who was suddenly seated at a fully laden banquet table.

Her lips, with that flawless bow, called to him.

Kiss me. Kiss me.

"Okay."

Her mouth rounded slightly as she spoke. The tiny

movement of her lips fascinated him. If he hadn't been ogling her so closely, he'd have missed it.

Had she read his mind? Had she sensed his need? Was she somehow agreeing to the desperate urges whispering through his brain? Thundering through his veins? Was she urging him to kiss her?

No. No. That just couldn't be.

Without even thinking about it, he pulled his hand away from the back of her neck.

Amy tensed immediately, and that set off a small chain reaction: her head dipped backward, she flung out her arms and a gasp issued from her throat. Automatically he grasped her upper arm. She thrashed in the water until she could get her feet beneath her.

Sputtering and coughing, she laughed as she scrubbed her hand over her face.

"I thought I was ready." She flicked water from her fingertips. "But I...I guess I wasn't."

Their gazes collided like two comets flying through space. The amusement that had struck her left her in a breathy rush. Jolting electricity swirled about them, permeating them, igniting the air with a prickly current that was nearly tangible.

They didn't speak. Didn't breathe.

Droplets glistened like diamonds along the line of her cheekbone. He felt as if time was shifting into a lower gear. He lifted his hand and smoothed away the beads of water with a feathery swipe of his fingertips. Her bottom lip was velvet against the pad of his thumb. He stroked the full length of it, and desire sparked inside him like a blaze gone wild.

Her gaze never left his, the craving she felt darkening and intensifying her lovely mahogany eyes.

"My God, Amy," he whispered. "What *is* this?"

Chapter Five

What is *this*? he'd asked.

Attraction. Allure. *Lust.*

Before this moment, Amy would have used any and all of those terms to describe what she experienced when she was with Pierce, when the man merely entered her thoughts. But now she felt those words were not ample enough—not profound enough—to define what was haunting her like some indomitable wraith.

She'd spent her entire adulthood shunning everything that even hinted of becoming a temptation regarding the opposite sex. Erotic urges ensnared a woman just as surely as if they were the steel jaws of trap.

But *this*…

This was something…more. Something mysterious. Something that bordered on the ethereal. The unexplainable. The otherworldly. And she found it wholly entrancing.

The magnetism pulling her intensified when Pierce cupped her jaw with his hand and leaned toward her.

He's going to kiss me. The thought burst in her head like a neon sign in the darkest part of the night.

In that mindless instant there was nothing on earth Amy wanted more.

His gaze was steady as he slowly inched closer. She feared that, before she even had the chance to taste him, he was going to devour her whole with those feverish green eyes of his. Well, she was more than ready to be consumed.

His mouth slanted down over hers. His kiss was heart-wrenchingly tender, and Amy savored it. When his tongue skimmed lightly along her lips, she parted them, the invitation she offered as instinctive as breathing.

Answering her unspoken call, Pierce deepened the kiss…and Amy's head swam. She could feel the cool dampness of his hair, yet she didn't remember lifting her hand to weave her fingers through it.

The kiss intensified further, his arms pulling her tight, their thighs and torsos pressing together. Their tongues dancing, tasting, exploring. Amy felt that the outside world suddenly ceased to exist.

All she heard was the sound of Pierce's heavy breathing, and the whoosh of hot blood through her ears. All she smelled was the warm scent that was his alone. All she tasted was the faint salty tang of seawater on their lips. All she felt was the vivid pounding of her pulse at every pressure point in her body, the wet silk of his hair tangled in her fingertips, the solid length of his powerful body pressed full against her own….

And his lips against hers.

She'd have been happy to spend eternity right here, in his arms.

Her greatest wish at that moment was that this kiss would never end. This kiss that set her aflame. That caused her insides to churn with some never-before-experienced emotion. But the forever she was hoping for was short-lived, and the kiss ended. It wasn't that their separation had been the deliberate act of either one of them, but a simultaneous and oh-so-reluctant parting.

One look at the awe portrayed on his handsome face and she knew he was enduring the same feeling of total mystification as she. Both of them were over-whelmed to the point of mute confusion.

Pierce swallowed, blinked. He ran his tongue along his still-moist bottom lip, and, witnessing the move-ment, she was flooded with a renewed sense of yearn-ing. She had to force herself not to lean forward, re-turning to his warm embrace.

Finally he rasped, "What is this, Amy?"

He grasped, she realized, that whatever had taken control of them was something more than mere phys-ical need. Something more than simple desire.

Whatever this was that insisted on dominating them was complex. Insurmountable. Unexplainable. And completely discombobulating.

Even though the haze continued to fog her brain, panic sprouted to life. She wanted to run. She wanted to hide. However, she feared that no matter where she went, this...this *thing* would find her.

Better to face it head-on, she decided.

"I don't know what this is," she admitted, whispering the plain and honest answer to his question. Summoning some vitality into her tone, she continued, ''I thought I could fight it off. I thought I could control it.'' Her breath left her in a sigh. ''But I was wrong.''

''I know what you mean.'' He reached up and combed his wet hair straight back from his forehead. ''I felt the same. But Amy, if it's this strong…if it's this determined…maybe fighting it is the wrong strategy.''

What he said startled her into taking a backward step, the motion sending the water swirling in lazy concentric circles all about her. And that small increase in distance between them helped to clear her head a little more.

His eyes had turned all dreamy, and it made the normally analytical doctor all the more appealing to her. She got the distinct impression that he wasn't measuring the implications of what he said before he spoke. That he was simply voicing his thoughts as they formed in his head.

''I don't know what you're thinking—'' she shook her head adamantly ''—but I want no part of it. I've already told you that much.''

''But Amy—''

She backed up another step.

''In my line of work,'' he argued, ''it's always best to explore what you don't understand. Knowledge conquers fear. It always has. It always will.''

Insult had her spine straightening. ''I am not afraid.'' But then she pinched her bottom lip between her teeth. The need to restate her opinion welled up sharply, refusing to be ignored. "Well, on second thought, maybe I am."

She inched away from him farther, let her hands dip into the cool waters of the bay, gulped in a deep breath. However, even though the haze swimming around in her thoughts was slowly but surely dissipating, the offense stiffening her muscles and making her jaw tight refused to budge. "But if I do fear t-this *thing* between us, it's only because I've seen what it can do to a person."

Her emphasis of the nebulous entity wasn't made consciously. But for some reason she felt the need to identify the enemy—that thing that could destroy all her hopes and dreams. Even if she was unable to label it with a name.

Questions clouded his gaze. However, before he had the chance to ask a single one, the boys' laughter captured their attention. Amy turned to see them running across the lawn back toward the bay.

"We'll have to talk about this later," she told Pierce.

"Yes," he said. "We'll have to talk."

Amy entered the house by the front door, feeling refreshed after her long walk. The temperature had cooled with the setting sun, and she'd spent quite a while choosing the words she planned say to Pierce once they had a chance to discuss what had happened earlier.

"Amy! Amy!" The twins ran toward her as if they'd been caught up in a whirlwind. "Will you read us a bedtime story?"

"She most certainly will not."

Pierce came around the corner, and she felt her pulse quicken. He looked utterly handsome in his casual T-shirt and shorts. His legs were lean and tanned, his feet bare.

"You boys know it's Amy's day off," Pierce continued. "She's supposed to be getting a break from the likes of the three of us. I'll read to you."

"But we want Amy," Jeremiah lamented.

The boy's proclamation, and the expression it brought to Pierce's face, had Amy chuckling.

"It's okay," she told Pierce. "I don't mind reading them a book."

"Yeah!" Benjamin and Jeremiah performed a joyous dance around her.

Sensing that Pierce was about to object, Amy lifted her palm. "It really is okay. Honestly."

The couple of seconds that followed were a bit odd. He stared at her face, his eyes seeming to rove from her forehead to her chin.

Good, she thought. He was finally noticing her makeover…or should she call it her make*under*?

During her trip to the mall today, she'd purchased several new outfits, every single one of them as casual as the one she wore now. She'd selected shorts and simple cotton tops, canvas sneakers and a pair of plain, inexpensive sandals.

And the crucial piece in this new look? A face scrubbed free of makeup. No foundation. No eyeliner or shadow or mascara. No blush. No lipstick. Nothing that might make her look appealing to Pierce.

But he was attracted to you this afternoon, a haunting voice piped up from somewhere in the back of her brain. *Attracted enough to kiss you!*

That voice had niggled at her during her walk, too. But she'd succeeded in pooh-poohing it into silence, just as she did now.

In that playful, frolicking situation earlier in the bay, he simply hadn't yet noticed her transformation. However, she saw how he stared at her now—a frown planted deep in his brow—and she knew without a doubt that he was good and truly aware of the change in her appearance.

She lifted her chin, feeling as though she'd succeeded. Stripped of all the outward accoutrements that had made her feel professional—not to mention pretty—Amy realized Pierce would never find her the least bit provocative now.

However, that thought made her smile falter, and she inadvertently dipped her head as awkwardness descended upon her like a damp wool blanket.

Quickly, a renewed sense of purpose squared her shoulders. She didn't want Pierce to think she was pretty. That was the whole reason behind buying the casual attire and washing every trace of makeup off her face.

"Come on, boys," she said. *"Allons à la salle de toilette."*

"What's that?" Benjamin asked, the excitement of learning something new lighting his eyes.

"I said, 'Let's go to the bathroom,'" she translated. "You two have to brush your teeth before going to bed, right?" She chuckled, wanting desperately to shake off every nuance of the perturbing discomfort that had fallen over her. "You don't have to brush them all. Just the ones you want to keep."

The boys snorted.

"You speak French?" Pierce asked her.

Before she could answer, Jeremiah said, "She does! And Uncle Pierce, she's been teaching us. Wanna hear us count the steps as we go up 'em?"

"I'd love that."

Amy stood between the boys, the three of them clasping hands as they made their way up the stairs.

"Un, deux, trois, quatre…"

At this point Jeremiah stammered. Benjamin supplied *"cinq"* as they stepped up on the fifth riser. Then both boys went quiet.

"I think you're both doing a great job," Amy announced, "for only having practiced counting in French for a week." She turned to look down at Pierce. "Don't you think so?"

"I do."

Something was stewing in Pierce's gaze, something Amy wasn't able to name, but whatever it was it made her mighty uncomfortable. She looked from one of the boys to the other.

"Let's go! A story awaits." And the three of them hurried up the remaining steps. To Pierce she called, *"Au revoir."*

The silken summer night was lit by the warm glow of the strategically placed deck lights. While Amy had been upstairs reading to Benjamin and Jeremiah, Pierce had poured tall glasses of lemonade and had put some cheese and crackers on a plate. Amy filled his thoughts.

She was a marvel. She'd completely changed her look from professional chic to fresh and youthful and more-appealing-than-ever. She could laugh at herself, and had done so when she'd tensed up and sank like a rock during their swimming lesson. She spoke French. Surely there were thousands of other things about her…things he didn't know. Things he *wanted* to know.

He'd carried the refreshments out to the deck so they could talk there against the backdrop of the tranquil bay and the lushly blooming foliage. Amy stepped outside, and he turned his head from where he sat waiting.

"I've been looking for you."

He smiled. "You found me."

Something stirred the air. He felt the slight tremor, as if the atmosphere surrounding him was liquid and she'd disturbed its stillness by coming near. He perceived from the tentativeness in her dark eyes that she felt it, too.

She didn't want to have anything to do with this. She'd been clear about that on two different occasions now. But that didn't stop the attraction from existing.

He had wanted to ignore it, as well. He'd already decided to do so, for some very solid reasons. However, disregarding whatever it was between himself and Amy seemed an impossibility after the amazing kiss they had shared today, so the scientist in him had been urged to explore. To discover.

Science was concrete. If the unknown was thoroughly investigated, it could be dealt with. Solved. But for some reason Amy found that idea distressing.

And now, he thought as he looked at her, she intended to tell him why.

"Come," he coaxed her. "Sit. Let's talk." He took

the glasses of lemonade from the tray and offered one to her.

"Thank you." She took a sip, then looked off toward the horizon. "It sure was hot today."

In more ways than one, he wanted to respond. But he held his tongue.

"Would you rather go inside?" he asked. "We could sit at the kitchen table. Or in the den."

She shook her head. "The air seems to have cooled a little now that the sun has gone down." She sat, and now that the small talk seemed to have petered out, she looked quite discomfited.

"Look, Amy," he said, "we know what we want to discuss. We're both adults. There's no need to feel uncomfortable about this, or feel the need to ease into it. Let's just lay it out on the table. We're feeling…something. Something for one another. And we both agree that it seems to be more than mere physical attraction. It's…it's—" bewilderment forced a sigh from his lips "—something else."

Frustration over his inability to classify this mystery had the rest of his thought fading. Refusing to be daunted, he continued, "I suggested this afternoon that we do a little exploring, and you refused. This thing scares you. And you were about to tell me why when the boys interrupted our conversation."

She studied the icy yellow liquid in her glass, but he could see her delicate brows rising as he spoke. Finally, she lifted her chin and gazed into his face.

"Well, there certainly won't be any beating around the bush here, will there?" She grinned, and it was so rueful and sweet that he couldn't help but return it.

''I don't see why there should be.''

Her head bobbed. ''I agree with you. Like you said, we're adults.''

She went quiet. Then she took another sip from her glass, moisture making her bottom lip glisten enticingly. Like a two-by-four between the eyes, an errant thought hit him—how might that tart lemonade change the sweetness of those lips he'd tasted earlier today?

Pierce blinked and shoved the notion from his head.

Her sigh was heavy, as if she were about to embark on a long, arduous trip.

''I do want to tell you why,'' she began haltingly. ''Why this…thing frightens me.'' She paused, licked her lips.

He couldn't help but notice how her tongue had tripped over those last four words. This subject really was difficult for her.

It was awkward for him, too. But as he figured it, this conversation was necessary.

''You have to understand.'' Again she stared down into her glass. ''Lebo is a very, very small town. It doesn't have much to offer in the way of cultural experiences. I've wanted to leave—wanted to see what the rest of the world was like—ever since I can remember.''

Her tone took on a mellifluous, far-off quality, and Pierce's eyes latched onto her profile.

''My mother died when I was young,'' she continued. ''In a freak accident. She climbed a ladder to change a light bulb in one of the rooms of our motel.

She slipped and fell. Struck her head on the edge of a bathtub.''

He studied her face, saw that she seemed to detach herself from the story as she told it.

''My father had taken me to the store to pick up supplies.'' Another sigh issued from deep inside her. ''A man stopped in to rent a room for the night. No one was manning the front desk, so he went searching for someone to help him. Unfortunately for him, he found my mother's body.''

Sympathy made his heart pinch. However, he also found it curious that she recounted the tale with so little emotion.

''The sheriff contacted your brother-in-law,'' Amy went on. ''Reverend Winthrop found Dad at the hardware store. That's where Dad was told his wife had died. At Stover's Lumber and Hardware.''

Pierce hadn't realized that John had been living in Lebo, Kansas, during the time that Amy's mother had passed away. He hadn't known that his brother-in-law had been the one who broke the tragic news to Amy's father. Of course, this had to have been years before John and Cynthia had married.

For the first time, Pierce sensed Amy's sadness. He couldn't say why, but he got the distinct impression her sorrow was completely on her father's behalf, for losing his spouse, and not for herself for having lost her mother.

Suddenly Amy's dark eyes were full on him. ''I was too young to remember any of this. Too young, even, to retain any memories of my mother. Oh, I've heard stories of her from Dad. I have lots of pictures. But it's really hard to miss someone you've never really known. To connect with someone you can't remember. You know what I mean?''

She wasn't looking for an answer to her question, he knew. It was added on as a means of urging him to attempt to relate to her feelings, to her experience. And, surprisingly, he could.

His father might not have died during Pierce's youth, as Amy's mother had during hers, but the man hadn't been around much. So Pierce did understand just how hard it was to connect with someone you'd never really known.

He couldn't help but ask, ''Is that how…'' The rest of his question died away when he realized he didn't know Amy's father's name. ''What's your dad's name? Although I'm sure John has mentioned him and I should remember.''

''Eli,'' she provided. ''Eli Edwards.''

''Is that how Eli and John came to be such close friends?'' he asked.

''That's what Dad says,'' Amy told him. ''Dad never talks about Mom's death without mentioning how Reverend Winthrop stayed with him for hours every day, helping him through his grief.'' She shrugged. ''Like I said, I don't remember. But Dad has always been grateful to the reverend for what he did back then. I do have memories of Reverend Winthrop. I remember when he went away and then returned to Lebo with his young wife. Your sister. Of course, that was when I was older. In fact, my father and I went to the Winthrops' home once for Christmas dinner. It was hard to get away from the motel, though. A business like that has to be open all the time, holidays included, if you want to maintain your reputation for being reliable.''

Pierce nodded. Several seconds ticked by and it seemed as if she was deep in thought. Then another question compelled him to speak. ''Amy, how does this fit in with what we wanted to talk about? How does losing your mother—''

''Let me finish,'' she said, her voice whisper soft. ''I'll put it all together for you.''

He pressed his lips together in an unspoken oath of silence.

''I—I love my mother.'' She stammered over the words. ''I guess what I love is the memory of her that my father has tried to offer me. But I truly love my dad. I'm dedicated to him. He worked so very hard to keep me with him.

''I attended school with a girl whose mother died. Her father shipped her off to live with her grandmother. But not my dad. He wanted us to be together. He did everything in his power to see that things went that way, too.''

Eli Edwards shared a tight father-daughter bond with Amy. That was evident.

''My dad never took a vacation. The motel was open weekdays, weekends, holidays. And in order to turn a profit, he did most of the work himself. Eventually I was able to help him.''

Again her eyes swung from the horizon to his face. ''This is an important part of my story, because my dad is the reason I, um, the reason I made the choices I made.''

She blanched, swallowed, looked away. But then her gaze rose to his again. He found her reaction to her own statement rather odd, but the thought drifted from his mind quickly enough.

"What I mean is, my dad is the reason I stayed in Lebo for as long as I did." She straightened in the chair. "I wanted to get out. But I stayed. In order to help Dad with the motel."

Okay. He got it. She had some desires for her life. To do some traveling. To experience the world outside her small hometown. However, she had put her own wants on hold out of her devotion for her father. But Pierce still didn't understand why that would make her want to shy away from exploring this phenomenal *something* that they felt when they were together.

He resolved to keep quiet for now. She'd said she'd put it all together for him. He trusted that she'd complete the puzzle before she finished.

"I watched my friends," she told him. "I saw, firsthand, the mistakes they made."

Her tone changed, grew resolved.

"One by one, they met men. Got married. Had kids. Soon they were so weighed down with responsibility, mortgage payments, car payments, doctor bills, credit debt, so stuck in the mire, that they could never get out from under it all even if they'd wanted to."

Ah, Pierce thought. Now they were getting to the meat of the tale.

"I knew that one day I'd have my chance. One day I'd be free to do what I wanted. Go where I wanted. See all the things I'd been longing to see. And that time came just last year."

Her shoulders were square, her spine straight, excitement lighting her nutmeg eyes.

"A large corporation offered to buy my father out," Amy explained. "They wanted to build a hotel on what they said was our prime piece of property. My father refused at first. He said that the motel was mine. That he wanted to hand it down to me. To offer me a means of making a living for the rest of my life." She paused. "That's when I finally had to be honest with him. And it was the hardest thing I've ever done."

Judging from the pain that eclipsed her sudden bout of exhilaration, Pierce could see that she was speaking the truth.

"I told him that running the motel wasn't my life's ambition." She frowned. "He was hurt. And that about killed me. But I had to tell him, Pierce. I had to. Otherwise, I'd have been just as stuck as my friends were."

He set down the glass he was holding. He wanted to reach out to her, but decided that it wasn't a good idea. So instead he murmured, "I understand."

Appreciation tinted the small smile she offered him.

"Dad was really quiet for several days," she continued. "But he came around. In fact, he was the one who suggested I apply for a job as a flight attendant. 'What better way to see the world?' he said. I'd be traveling all over and getting paid to do it. So that's what I did. I got a job with an airline. I completed my training. This ear problem may have postponed my maiden voyage—" a smile hovered at the edges of her mouth "—but as soon as my health is cleared

at the end of the summer, I'll be off on the first metal
bird that's flying out."

When she talked about seeing the world, her whole
face seemed to take on a thrilled glow.

"So, you see, I can't be messing around with—"
She stopped short when it was obvious that she
couldn't come up with a name for what it was between them. "Well, with any of this kind of stuff."
She waved her hand between the two of them to in-
dicate the topic of their discussion. "It's my turn to
live the life of my dreams. I've sacrificed for years. I
can't risk anything holding me back, Pierce. I *won't*
risk it."

Chapter Six

Curiosity killed the cat. That idiom hadn't come into being without good and sound reason. Inquisitiveness was known to get people into deep trouble. Throughout history, the inability to leave things be had caused entire kingdoms to fall. Amy feared that curiosity was going to get the best of her, too.

She watched Jeremiah and Benjamin hard at work at the play table in their room, applying waxy color to the pictures they were carefully drawing for their parents. Amy had taken to boxing up care packages for John and Cynthia Winthrop—cards, letters, snapshots, small gifts and homemade goodies. The practice made the twins happy, made them feel as if they were doing something wonderful for their mom and dad, and made the boys feel closer to them. The boys were working on pictures to include in this week's care package as Amy's mind wandered.

It had been two long weeks since she had explained

to Pierce her reasons for needing to avoid the heady magnetism that pulsed between them. She felt confident that he understood her motivation. However, the end of the conversation continued to run through her mind, continued to stir her curiosity.

He'd remained silent for some time after she'd finished talking that night. Then, without taking his green eyes off her face, he'd nodded somberly.

"I'd thought that doing a bit of exploring might help us to better understand what's happening between us," he'd told her. "That if we understood it, we could better control it. But I can see that's not something you want to do. And I fully understand why now. I'll respect your wishes, Amy. In fact, I have some really strong reasons of my own for steering clear of…this thing." He'd pressed his palms to his knees, then stood. There had been deep conviction in his tone as he'd summed up. "So we're going to disregard what we're feeling. Act as if it's not there. If that's what you want, I can do it."

And that had been the last they'd spoken of the matter.

I have some really strong reasons of my own.

Those words kept echoing in her brain. Any normal person would be poked and prodded by the need to know what those reasons might be, and she certainly categorized herself as normal. As each day passed, the desire to know what motivated Pierce to ignore what was between them had niggled at her until she was now burning with inquisitiveness.

She shouldn't care. But she did. She wanted to know. She wanted to hear why he wanted to avoid love—

BUSINESS REPLY MAIL

FIRST-CLASS MAIL   PERMIT NO. 717-003   BUFFALO, NY

POSTAGE WILL BE PAID BY ADDRESSEE

SILHOUETTE READER SERVICE
3010 WALDEN AVE
PO BOX 1867
BUFFALO NY 14240-9952

NO POSTAGE
NECESSARY
IF MAILED
IN THE
UNITED STATES

No! Love was *not* what they were dodging. The thing they were desperate to evade was *the chance* of something like that happening. The chance that their relationship might grow into something beyond mere friendship.

There was a difference—a small nuance of a difference, maybe, but a difference nonetheless—and she clung to it.

She'd explained her motivation for avoiding the overwhelming desires he stirred in her. So what were his reasons?

There simply was no way to safely broach the subject that wouldn't make her seem…interested. The last thing she wanted, now that the two of them had established firm boundary lines regarding the incredible feelings they spurred in each other, was to come off looking too interested in him.

But wasn't that exactly what she was? Interested in him?

In his past, maybe. In the experiences he'd had that would have made him decide to avoid man-woman relationships. But she wasn't interested in him in any way other than that.

Liar, a tiny voice taunted from the back of her brain. A voice that at first had been fairly easily banished ever since their talk on the deck. But as the days wore on, the murmurings in her head were asserting themselves into her conscious thoughts more and more. Becoming stronger and less easy to wrestle into submission.

She sensed him standing at the door of the boys' room. There was no need to glance over her shoulder—she felt the zing in the air, the slight change in the temperature of the room. The tiny hairs on her arms stood on end and she fought the urge to run her hands over the gooseflesh that broke out on her skin in his presence.

"Uncle Pierce." Benjamin called a greeting. "Come look what I drew for Mommy and Daddy!"

"I drew a picture, too," Jeremiah said.

After inhaling a fortifying breath, she cast Pierce a quick look. He nodded a greeting, and she returned it. This small gesture had become their routine salutation. It was innocent. Innocuous. Safe. All things they both needed.

The swirling enigma had entered the room along with him like a physical being. She sensed it just as surely as she was aware of the breeze blowing in through the window, sun-warmed and tinged with a hint of the sea. It might be invisible, but it was intent on making itself known.

Pierce walked to the table and peered down at the boys' artwork.

"That's great, guys," he told them.

Benjamin pointed to his picture. "Here's the house. Here's me and you and Jeremiah and Amy."

"We're in the bay," Pierce observed.

"Yeah, I drew a picture of you teaching all of us to swim. I drew this for Mommy and Daddy so they'd know we're having a good time together."

There had been a small hitch with the swimming lessons. The boys had continued on with theirs, but Amy had thought it best if she made her excuses. Benjamin and Jeremiah had been disappointed, of course, but Pierce hadn't given the least argument. Because of this fact, a new rule had been put into place—the boys didn't go into the bay without their uncle present.

Pierce squatted down to get closer to Benjamin. He placed his hand on the boy's shoulder. "I think it's a great picture. Your parents are going to love it."

"How about mine?" Jeremiah held up the piece of construction paper. "Can you guess what it is?"

"Ah," Pierce said, studying the image intently. "That's a *callinectes sapidus.*"

"A call-in-*what*?" Jeremiah's brow bunched, his tongue tripping over the scientific term. "Uncle Pierce, don't you see the claws? They're blue. And those beady eyes? This is a Maryland blue crab."

Pierce chuckled. "That's what I said, Jeremiah. I just gave you the name of the species. *Callinectes* is Greek. It means 'beautiful swimmer.' And *sapidus* is Latin for 'tasty.'"

The child continued to look perplexed. "I don't know that I'd call a blue crab beautiful, but—" he shrugged "—they are pretty tasty when they're seasoned just right."

Pierce ruffled his nephew's hair and grinned.

Awareness crackled around Amy like static electricity. Her eyes traveled over Pierce's body. His face and arms were tanned golden-brown from the extra time he'd been taking each afternoon to play with the boys out in the yard, and his powerful thigh muscles strained against the fabric of his cotton trousers as he squatted by the table.

Amy's mouth went dry, and she attempted to keep her gaze on the plastic container filled with crayons. She concentrated on them, noticing the preferred, well-used bits that had lost their paper wrappers, as well as the odd-hued ones that still looked new.

Yet time and again her eyes darted to Pierce as he interacted with the children.

The mocking voice in her brain chose that instant to whisper, *With his raven's-wing hair and those intense green eyes, he sure would make some pretty babies.*

A gasp gathered in her throat. Her brows rose. Her eyes widened. But it took only a moment of grappling with her reaction before she got it under control. Thankfully, no one seemed to notice.

"Amy helped us bake cookies this morning," Benjamin told his uncle.

"We're going to pack 'em up with these pictures and mail 'em off to Mommy and Daddy," Jeremiah added.

"Well, I hope you saved a cookie or two for me." Pierce balanced himself by placing a hand on the table's edge.

Her gaze latched onto his tapered fingertips, remembering how his touch sparked fire in her. But then she lowered her eyelids and took a deep breath, and when she opened her eyes again, she forced herself to think only about the conversation at hand.

"Oh, don't worry 'bout that!" Jeremiah's smile was so big, the small scar on his chin stretched taut. "We made a double batch."

The boy's excitement was infectious and she found herself grinning right along with him.

"Amy said that we'll have to pack the cookies just right so they don't break." Benjamin's expression grew serious. "I don't want Daddy's cookies to arrive in Africa all crumbled up. That wouldn't be good at all.''

"Don't worry, hon," Amy assured him. "We'll protect them."

Her heart warmed. She couldn't help but imagine how John and Cynthia Winthrop would feel when they received the pictures their sons had drawn for them, when they tasted the cookies the boys had spent time baking just for them to enjoy. Amy would like to think that someday she just might have a son or daughter who would make small gifts…just for her and the man she might someday call husband.

Again her eyes drifted to Pierce, and he chose that moment to look her way. Their gazes caught. And held.

For the duration of three heartbeats she felt as if she'd never in her life experienced such power. Finally it became too much to bear.

Immediately she dipped her chin and stared down at her hands where they were fisted in her lap.

What was the matter with her? She had hopes. She had plans. Dreams of seeing the world. Dreams of encountering different people, different places. Dreams that were so close to being realized she could almost see them and taste them.

The time for marrying and having babies, if it happened at all, was years away for her. Years away.

How far in the future was that time for Pierce? The question flooded her mind as if a dam had broken, filling every nook and cranny with curiosity, making her feel as if she would drown in it. Was he putting off marriage and children just for the time being? Or was he thinking of never marrying? Never fathering kids?

Frustration churned in her stomach like hot acid. Yes, curiosity was really going to get her into deep trouble. She could feel it in her bones.

Why? *Why* were thoughts of his man haunting her so?

"Amy?"

The rich timbre of his voice caressed her. Soothed her as surely as if it were a cool cloth against feverish flesh. She inhaled deeply not daring to lift her eyes to his just yet. She didn't want him to know what she was feeling, and she suspected that those intense eyes of his, that quick intelligence, would surely figure out that she was once again in turmoil...all because of him.

"You seem disturbed about something."

She smiled at him then, imposing a calmness on her countenance that was directly opposed to the emotions seething inside her.

"I'm fine," she said, satisfied that her tone sounded somewhat serene. "I'm wondering, though," she continued, "what you're doing home so early? You usually work until dinnertime."

"I thought we'd go out to eat tonight." Then he looked at the boys. "How do hamburgers and French fries sound?"

Both boys cheered their approval.

Amy *tsked*. "That wouldn't be a very healthy dinner."

"You can have a salad." The suggestion seemed to spill from Benjamin without thought. Jeremiah snickered and Pierce laughed.

"Yeah," Pierce agreed. "You can have a salad."

She put forth a long-suffering sigh, but the light-heartedness of the moment got to her. She chuckled. "Who in their right mind would eat lettuce when everyone else is enjoying fat, juicy hamburgers and French fries smothered in ketchup?"

Raising both hands heavenward, Jeremiah gleefully added, "With *extra* ketchup!"

Just forty-five minutes later, Amy and Pierce sat at the table in a small family-style eatery waiting for their order to be served. The boys were within sight, dropping quarters into video games.

The homey scents wafting in the air—hints of smoky bacon, grilling steak and fried onions—did nothing to calm Amy's agitation.

Pierce had his elbows resting on the table, his fingers steepled in front of his face. Lively background music filled the air, and he tapped his index fingers to the beat as he casually looked about him.

How could the man act so darned unruffled? The allure that had been spinning its web around them since he'd entered the boys' room and suggested they all go out to dinner had her feeling tangled in its pulsing energy. Coping with that was one thing, but the urge to ask him that burning question about his motivation for ignoring the very thing that had her all tangled up was pushing her to the very edge of reason.

"*Unruffled?*"

Amy's gaze flew to his face. "Pardon?"

His black brows arched high with what looked to

be incredulity and he asked, "You honestly think I look unruffled?"

Words failed her as a cyclone of panic swept through her entire being. Had she really uttered that question aloud? She knew she was completely off-kilter, but was she so vexed that she could voice a thought without even realizing it?

Apparently so.

That mouth of his, the one that was already as sexy as red-hot sin, pulled into a languorous smile that made her fear she'd drool.

"Then I guess I'm doing an excellent job of keeping our pact, aren't I?"

The man was definitely satisfied with himself. His powerful shoulders had squared, his hard chest had expanded a fraction, even his mouth had taken on a smug twist. If she hadn't been feeling so tense she'd have teased him, had a chuckle at his expense over his obvious puffing up.

However, in the blink of an eye his whole demeanor changed. His lips went flat, his jaw grew taut and his eyes…his eyes turned on her with a concentrated emotion that was simply too intense for her to tolerate. She had to look away.

But his palm smoothed over the back of her hand, calling her attention, and her gaze was drawn back to his like metal to a strong magnet.

"I'm feeling anything but." His voice was hushed. Ragged, even. "And I've been feeling anything but ever since our decision to ignore what's between us."

He paused as if to let his words sink in.

"Take this very moment, for instance. I've been

sitting here choking back the urge to tell you how beautiful you look.''

"Yeah, right.'' If manners hadn't mattered to her, she'd have snorted her disbelief at him.

His fingers squeezed hers. "I've noticed the change, Amy. You've gone...I don't know how to describe it...casual. Without all that makeup, your skin looks like a ripe peach. And your hair. The way it swings around your shoulders. It catches the light. Invites a man to touch it. Run his fingers through it.''

He stopped suddenly, chagrin tingeing his cheeks, and Amy got the impression that he'd gotten carried away with his description.

Pierce continued, "All I meant to say was that I've noticed your new look.'' He moistened his lips before adding, "And I like it. A lot.''

And here she'd been thinking that she'd succeeded with her transformation, that her reverse makeover made her something close to dowdy.

"You weren't supposed to like it.''

One corner of his mouth quirked a smidgen. "Ah, so the change *was* for me. I'd been obsessing over why you'd do away so completely with the Ms Professional image.''

Mild ire—make that pure unadulterated embarrassment at having been found out—made her attempt to pull her hand from underneath his, but he tightened his grip, a chuckle rumbling from deep in his chest.

"Hold on, now,'' he crooned. "Don't be angry. You have to admit that the Amy sitting here now is quite different from the one who first arrived at the house a month ago.''

She'd admit nothing. Especially the fact that she'd

changed her physical appearance for him. It was true, of course, but she didn't have to put herself through the humiliation of actually stating it.

"You said I look unruffled." He shrugged and grinned. "I think it's important for you to understand that I've been obsessed with...the new you."

Pleasure nearly had her toes curling. She didn't want to be delighted by all he was admitting. But she'd be lying if she said she wasn't.

"Speaking of obsessed..." Changing the subject, she decided, was her best course of action. "I've been quite fixated on something myself."

Keen interest sparked his dark gaze and his brows waggled up and down. "Fixated, huh? I like the sound of that."

Rolling her eyes at him, Amy tugged her fingers free from his. "Would you please be serious? I have a question."

Again he leveled that concentrated energy on her, and the congealed air was so thick she felt as if she would suffocate.

His gaze lingered momentarily on her mouth. "I'm as serious as leaf blight."

When she whispered his name her tone was brimming with warning. If he kept this up, her resistance to him—to this thing between them—would surely slip a notch.

Her heart beat once, twice, and just when she thought he meant to persist in churning up the sensuous atmosphere, his shoulders relaxed, his gaze calmed and his lips curled into an easy smile.

"Okay, I'll stop. But I want you to know I'm doing so against my will."

Oh, Lord above, so was she.

"So what's your question?"

Struck with sudden inhibition, she drew in on herself; she slid back in the seat, tucked her elbows close to her body and dipped her chin close to her chest. Now that she'd succeeded in veering off the risqué path he'd attempted to pave, she was shell-shocked to think that she'd so recklessly revealed to him that there was something about him that consumed her.

He consumed her, of course. But she'd been battling that. With every ounce of her strength. And she'd continue to do so, too.

Looking up at his handsome face through lowered lashes, she could see that Pierce was doing his darndest to rein in his emotions.

He'd been surprised that she thought he was in control—unaffected by their situation—and he'd quickly set her straight. The things he'd revealed to her and the sexual aura that he'd so swiftly whipped up were proof that he was engaged in a combat as fierce as her own.

So what did it matter if he discovered that the whys of his war interested her? It didn't, she decided.

Her inhalation was slow, bolstering, and she lifted steady eyes to his. She prefaced her inquiry with a tiny smile meant more to assure herself than him.

"Well," she began, "when we talked that night out on the deck...I told you about my goals, and how I felt it was my turn to reach for my dreams, and that I didn't want anything to get in the way of those things happening...."

He nodded.

"I was honest with you about the reasons I felt we

needed—'' for a moment she was at a loss for words, but then it came to her ''—the p-pact we made.''

''You were.''

One of her shoulders rose a fraction. ''So I've been wondering about yours. Your reasons, that is, for wanting…o-our pact.''

It was disquieting that her tongue continued to trip over the description of their situation. But she guessed that couldn't be helped.

''My reasons? You've been *fixated* on my reasons?''

The manner in which he enunciated the word sent a delicious chill coursing over her skin. He was baiting her, trying to stir up that sensual air again. But she refused to allow him to lure her.

Finally he chuckled. ''Okay, okay.'' He relented. ''I'll keep to the topic.''

His low, sexy laughter made her smile. ''Thank you. I'd appreciate that very much.''

This game they were toying with made her feel light and airy inside, and it was loads of fun. But she also knew it was highly dangerous.

Pierce sighed, absently picking up the paper napkin that sat at his place setting. Directing his gaze to the small candle in the center of the table, its golden flame flickering warmly, he said, ''My reason is solitary. It's my father. Or rather, the fact that I resemble him too closely for my liking.''

The motivations that drove him had had her thinking, wondering, for two weeks now. She'd imagined him having been hurt by a first love, or betrayed by a woman to whom he'd given his heart.

But she'd never imagined that his reason might involve his father. The one time Pierce had mentioned the man, he'd spoken with a bitterness that had set her mind to wondering. His statement that he resembled his father, someone for whom he obviously had ill feelings, only had her feeling bewildered, and she was certain that her face expressed just that.

"My father," he haltingly continued, "wasn't much of a parent. He was a brilliant man. An acclaimed scientist. And I admired him. Looked up to him. Like any boy would. But I was always looking for something from him that he was unable to give."

Seconds ticked by, and Amy could feel the anxiety vibrating around him, off him. She worried that he might be unable to continue. But then he curled his fingers into fists and tucked them beneath the table, leveling his gaze on her face.

He clarified. "Paternal love. Fatherly involvement. He left me feeling lacking in so many areas—concern, affection, protection. In every way, really, that a father can fail, mine did.

"My sister feels the same way. Cynthia and I have talked about it over the years. Our father wasn't there for us." A muscle in his jaw jerked. "He wasn't there for our mother, either."

He released the napkin, rested one elbow on the table again and curled his fingers lightly under his chin. "Mom loved the bastard. Even though he didn't deserve it. Never, in all my days of growing up here, did I see him reach out to her. Offer her a single demonstration of affection."

Reaching up, he combed his fingers through his hair.

"I'm sure my parents had a physical relationship,"

he said. The sound he emitted could have been described as laughter, but it held not an ounce of humor. "At least twice, anyway."

In any other circumstance, the quip would have made Amy smile.

"My mother was the only parent Cynthia and I ever knew. She took us to our club meetings, to school events and sporting practices. She helped us with our homework. She did everything in her power to give me and my sister happy, normal upbringings."

The solemnity that shadowed his green eyes deeply affected Amy.

"My father," Pierce told her, "was always too busy in the lab, or in the greenhouse, or off at some symposium presenting his findings, or accepting some reward, or talking some company CEO into funding his next new project.

"He didn't have time for us. He never wanted us. He didn't want to be a husband. And he sure didn't want to be a father."

The agitation bombarding him made the very air around them quiver. She felt it just as surely as if someone had taken the laminated menu and waved it in front of her face.

"He was a selfish, self-centered workaholic who couldn't make time for a family." Pierce heaved a sigh before he continued. His eyes were riveted on hers as he proclaimed, "And I'm just like him."

Chapter Seven

Amy came awake knowing something wasn't right. She sat up in the darkness of her room, listening. Something—she couldn't say what—had her tossing back the sheet, planting her feet on the carpet and reaching for her robe.

As she headed for the bedroom door she heard muffled sounds that she guessed were coming from the boys' room next door.

The hallway was dark as she slipped from her room. The fat summer moon streamed in through the window, casting a luminous glow over Benjamin and Jeremiah in their beds. Benjamin pitched, his head jerking from side to side as he muttered in his sleep.

Amy hurried to him, put her hand on his arm and gently shook him out of the depths of his disturbing slumber.

The child's gaze was wide, his chest heaving.

"Oh, honey," Amy crooned in a whisper. "You having a bad dream?"

"It was chasing me." Benjamin fisted the sleep from his eyes.

"Well, the dream is over now. You're safe. You can turn over and go back to sleep."

Alarm furrowed his brow. "I don't want to go back to sleep. Stay with me, okay?"

"Of course, sweetheart." Then she suggested, "Let's go downstairs for some milk. That way we won't disturb your brother."

Benjamin quickly scrambled from the tangle of his light cotton blanket and puttered across the room, Amy close on his heels. She took a quick peek at a sleeping Jeremiah before she pulled the bedroom door closed behind her.

Down in the kitchen, Amy poured a few inches of milk into two glasses and brought them over to the table. She set one down in front of Benjamin and then slid into the chair adjacent to his.

"Where do bad dreams come from, anyway?" His tone conveyed that the experience had him quite scared.

Amy smiled. "I guess they're like…well, stories. Stories that your mind makes up."

"I didn't like that story. A big dog was chasing me. Stringy slobber was hanging from his jaws. His teeth were bared. And big. And sharp." He picked up his glass and took a slug of milk.

"We saw dogs at the park today," she said. "Were you afraid of them?"

He lifted his face to hers, sporting a white mustache.

"No." He swiped at his upper lip with the back of his hand. "Those puppies were little. They were runnin' all around chasin' that ball. I had fun watchin' 'em.''

She reached out and patted his forearm. ''Well, the puppies in the park today probably planted the idea of a dog in your head. But there could be any number of reasons for your mind to turn your day of fun into a scary dream.''

He moved the glass and the milk sloshed a little, but his young features were focused on Amy's face.

''You could have been overtired when you went to bed,'' she continued. ''If you're upset or feeling stressed, that could bring on a bad dream, too.''

Benjamin was quiet, contemplative. And when he lifted his chin, his dark eyes glistened. In a tight, rusty tone, he admitted, ''I was thinking of Mommy today.''

He was doing all he could to keep his wits about him.

''I miss her.''

''I know you do, honey. It's very normal that you would think about her and miss her.''

Benjamin sniffed. ''I miss her hugs. And she always smells so good.''

Empathy radiated through Amy.

He turned his head, evidently embarrassed by the things he'd revealed. But then he swung to face her again, his gaze suddenly reckless. ''Mommy lets me sit on her lap. A-and I was thinkin' today that…that when she gets back I want to sit on her lap for a whole hour, and I don't care if Jeremiah makes fun of me or not.''

A knot rose in Amy's throat. She was afraid that

emotion would cause the words she wanted to say to come out all wobbly.

"I know I'm not your mom, honey, but I'd be happy to hug you anytime. And I have a lap, too, you know. You're welcome to sit on my lap. Of course, it wouldn't really be the same...."

The boy looked sorely tempted, and she pulled her chair back, opening her arms.

After only a moment's hesitation, he slid from his seat. "I don't think we should tell Jeremiah about this," he told her quite matter-of-factly, letting Amy pull him up against her chest. "He might think I'm a baby."

"Oh, he wouldn't think that. Everyone needs a hug now and then."

She wrapped her arms around him tightly and he settled into a comfortable position, his head cradled against her shoulder, his little body warm against hers. Amy cuddled his forehead with her cheek, smelled the clean scent of his freshly shampooed hair. She kissed his temple.

Instinctively she began to rock and hum.

The achy feeling behind her breastbone startled her. Over the weeks she'd been caring for Benjamin and Jeremiah she'd truly enjoyed herself. However, she was learning that these boys were wiggling their way into her most tender emotions.

That Benjamin would accept her offer of comfort in his mother's stead amazed her. It made her feel about ten feet tall and as if her heart had expanded beyond its normal bounds.

Motherhood.

Amy had always thought of it as a dirty word.

Something that would keep her from coming and going as she pleased. Something that would stifle her goals and aspirations.

She'd watched as one after another of her friends had become pregnant, become trapped in a situation that Amy had always imagined to be tedious and dull.

Her eyes drifted closed and she pressed her nose against Benjamin's warm skin.

Did those women back in Lebo know something she did not? An odd feeling stirred inside her, and she couldn't help but think that they just might have a clearer understanding of something that had always been beyond her grasp.

Until this moment.

Imagining herself with children of her own wasn't at all difficult while she cradled this sweet boy in her arms. Benjamin's breathing had become slow and measured, and she realized he'd fallen asleep.

She should take him back to his room and tuck him into bed. But she didn't move. Cuddling him was a joy.

Being a mother, she was beginning to think, would be a job filled with bliss and fascination. Experiencing life through the eyes of an inquisitive child was amazing. At least, that's what she'd experienced over these past weeks. She remembered being with the boys as the three of them had explored the bay, read stories, drawn pictures, baked cookies and brownies. Amy had been overwhelmed, time and again, by the quirky and often innocently wise observations expressed by the twins.

Of course, there was work involved. Lots of it. But she was starting to see that the good impacts and ex-

periences of having children in your life far out-
weighed the bad.

Comforting Benjamin, talking to him about his
nightmare, rocking him now were some of the most
satisfying moments of her life.

Amy couldn't help but think that she'd been wrong
in painting such a dim picture of parenthood, of family.

Family.

Most often that involved a man as well as a
woman. A husband and wife who shared a loving
relationship that resulted in blessings called children.
Thoughts of Pierce floated into her mind like a
brightly colored buoy bobbing on the still waters of
the bay, too conspicuous to be ignored.

If there was ever a man who might cause her to
reconsider her feelings regarding—

Before she could complete the thought, Pierce padded into the kitchen on bare feet. He paused suddenly,
obviously surprised to see her there.

"Is everything okay?"

Her heart thudded as she stared. Broad, bare shoulders. A sexy smattering of dark, springy chest hair.
Abdominal muscles that really did ripple—like those
on a model in some clothing ad in a glossy magazine—all the way down his torso until they disappeared beneath the low-slung waistband of his pajama
bottoms. The cotton cording was tied in a loose bow,
and Amy stopped herself from moistening her lips as
her eyes roved over the two knotted ends of the string
that dangled down low over his...

Her wide gaze made a beeline for his face, and she
made every effort to keep her smile from faltering.

He liked the fact that she noticed his body, that much was obvious even though he attempted to suppress the twinkle in his deep green eyes.

''B-Benjamin had a bad dream,'' she explained in a hushed tone. ''He was feeling a little anxious, so we came down to have a glass of milk until he felt a little better.''

Pierce approached them, placed one hand on her shoulder, smoothed the knuckles of his other hand across his nephew's forehead. ''Poor guy.''

The heat of his fingers penetrated the fabric of her robe. Her pulse accelerated and she turned her head.

His nails were trimmed neatly, his cuticles smooth. He let his hand hover on the curve of her shoulder, and for a moment she got the feeling he intended to let it glide up her neck, over her jaw.

Oh, *please!* The small voice in her head was chastising. She closed her eyes and gritted her teeth. When she lifted her lids, his hand was gone from her shoulder and he'd moved to the refrigerator.

''I was thirsty,'' he whispered.

He poured himself a glass of juice and drained it as he stood there with the fridge door open, its bulb casting a wedge of brightness on him that reminded Amy of a spotlighted actor on a stage.

The house was so quiet this time of the night. She heard him swallow, watched the muscles beneath his swarthy skin shudder. An image flashed in her head, unbidden—of her rising and sauntering over to him, taking the glass from his hand, running her tongue along the length of his throat.

The compulsion to taste Pierce's flesh was so strong she could actually picture herself surrendering to it. Her heart skittered, her blood rushed. Thank heaven above she was weighed down with Benjamin in her arms to the point that she couldn't easily stand. With a sigh she directed her gaze to the floor.

She heard him return the juice to the shelf and close the refrigerator door. His bare feet came into her line of view.

He knelt beside her, and when she didn't immediately lift her gaze to his, he tipped up her chin with gentle fingers.

"This is an amazing thing, Amy. An amazing thing."

His voice stroked her. Tugged at her. But she remained stubbornly silent, refusing to respond to his observation because she wasn't sure what he was referring to. The desire pumping through her was amazing, but she hadn't said a word, hadn't uttered a sound, so how could he know?

When it became clear to him that she was determined not to respond to his remark, he whispered, "Thanks for caring about the boys. You've been there for them in a way I never could."

Pierce reached up then and lightly touched the strand of hair that fell across her cheek, pushing it back from her face.

She couldn't speak. Didn't dare.

"Here," he said to her, "I'll take him."

His hands and arms contacted her briefly as he scooped Benjamin against him and then stood. He walked to the kitchen doorway and then turned back to her, a smile curving his mouth.

"I think you should know," he quipped softly,

''you looked quite natural sitting there with Benjamin on your lap.''

Pleasure bolted though her like lightning, shocking and unexpected. Followed close on its heels was a walloping affront.

''Don't sound so surprised.'' She followed him from the room, toward the stairs. ''Every woman has maternal instincts, you know.''

He ignored her, silently trudging up the steps.

Yes, every woman had it in her to comfort children who were sad. To protect children who were in trouble. Motherly instincts.

It just so happened that she'd discovered hers while living under Pierce's roof. However, no matter how soft and mushy those maternal impulses caused her heart to become, she sure didn't intend to cultivate them.

She had plans, damn it. She'd sacrificed plenty. Sacrificed in ways that Pierce didn't even know about.

She fully intended to take her turn at life.

''So what was it like?'' Pierce had been sitting next to her for a good ten minutes now, and he couldn't stand the silence a moment longer.

He'd found Amy watching the boys play in the backyard. She'd dug out several old sheets, some heavy twine and a few old boxes, and Jeremiah and Benjamin were busy building a structure while she sat under the shade of the oak tree.

''What was what like?''

''Growing up without a mother,'' he supplied.

She didn't answer right away, only gazed at him

with those rich nutmeg eyes of hers. Sudden anxiety welled. Was his question too probing? Too personal?

However, the slight unease he suffered didn't stem his curiosity. He honestly wanted to know.

"I haven't offended you, have I?" he asked.

She shook her head, but remained silent.

In the hopes of getting her to cast off her inhibitions of talking about her childhood, he offered, "My mother was such a huge part of my life when I was a boy. It's hard for me to imagine growing up without her."

One of her shoulders rose the merest fraction of an inch. "You don't miss what you don't know, Pierce."

"You said your father provided you with some memories."

This produced a smile on her lovely lips.

"He did," she said. "He had pictures. Of their wedding. Of my birth. Of special occasions." She paused, and when she continued, her tone took on a feathery quality. "Dad talked about Mom a lot. She was definitely the love of his life."

"He never remarried?"

Her long hair fell over her shoulder when she shook her head in answer. "I never really gave it a thought." One corner of her mouth twitched. "No little girl wants her daddy to remarry. But now that I'm older, I see that my dad never had a chance to even meet another woman. He worked so hard keeping the motel running."

"I think you worked hard, too," he pointed out.

"I did. But there's nothing wrong with that, is there? Hard work keeps a kid out of trouble."

He chuckled. "True. But there are other ways of

that happening. Sports. Clubs. School. How did you like school? What were your favorite courses?''

"Benjamin!" She shifted in the lawn chair as she called out. "Don't play too rough."

The glance she tossed Pierce's way barely skimmed his face before she looked back out at the boys.

"I asked them if they wanted my help," she said. "But they said Knights of the Round Table didn't need help building a castle."

Pierce laughed. "Ah, boys of all ages love King Arthur."

"Yes, we've been reading a children's version of the story." She grinned. "I fully expected them to ask me to play a princess in distress."

"A princess you could pull off without a hitch," he said. "But what will you do if they ask you to become a dragon?"

Now she chuckled, and Pierce liked the sound of it. Very much.

"Oh, if they caught me on the right day, I could manage that."

He stretched out his legs in front of him. "I find that hard to believe. I've never seen you act the least bit dragonish."

"Stick around. You'll soon find out that I'm a woman of many moods."

Pierce knew he wouldn't mind witnessing each and every one of them.

Sunlight filtered down through the lush greenery overhead, dappling her tanned and shapely legs. He let his eyes travel down the full length of them.

A couple of minutes passed and he realized she hadn't answered his question.

"So, you never said," he began, "how you liked school. Did you find all the subjects a breeze? Or were you more like me? Did you struggle with certain classes?"

"Everyone struggles," she said. "Don't you think?"

Then it seemed as if an errant thought popped into her head. She darted a quick look at her watch and blurted, "What are you doing out here, anyway? Shouldn't you be in your lab? Or in the greenhouse?"

He should. He had plenty of work to keep him busy. Plants that needed tending. Data that needed recording. But something kept pulling at him.

Something, hell. He knew what was tugging at his thoughts.

Amy. She was an extraordinary woman. And he wanted to spend time with her, experiments or no experiments.

The chuckle emanating from him sounded self-conscious. "You're not getting off that easy," he said in a valiant attempt to place the focus squarely on her and off himself. "So you found school a struggle, too, huh? Tell me what you remember."

She wrinkled her nose, and he thought the sight was cute. When she nibbled her bottom lip he got the strange notion that she was suddenly feeling nervous.

"I was pretty lucky—"

Once she started talking, she seemed to relax, and the idea that she was anxious faded from his mind.

"—where school was concerned." She shifted in her chair. "When my mother died, the whole town rallied around us. My father was approached by a group of Oblate Sisters who ran a primary parochial school. They offered me a free education, and my father gladly accepted. I attended preschool through eighth grade at the school. And it was a wonderful experience.''

The memory made her radiate.

''That was such a nice thing for the nuns to do.''

She nodded. ''It was. Those selfless women made such an impact on my life.''

''Oh?''

Her smile was warm. ''They made me read. A lot. The books they put in my hands let me know that there was a huge world out there just waiting to be explored.''

''I see. The sisters influenced your dreams to travel. At a very basic level.''

''Yes, they did. And they continued to encourage me for…years.''

The air took on a prickliness, and it seemed as if Amy couldn't decide what to focus on as her eyes darted like a butterfly flitting from flower to flower.

''As you can guess,'' she said, ''my favorite subjects were literature and languages. The French language, to be exact. It's so lyrical. Lucky for me, the sisters trained in France, so French was a required subject. I suppose your favorite subject was science.''

''Yeah.'' He was surprised by the ire in his tone. ''For all the good it did me.''

Her expression was proof that his aside surprised her as much as it did him.

''What's that supposed to mean?'' she asked.

He didn't know how to answer. He couldn't even

say what had spurred the statement, let alone what it might imply.

"Pierce, you didn't want to become a scientist?" Then it looked as if a light bulb went off in her pretty head. "You're in the field of plant research because of your father."

The statement hadn't contained one iota of accusation, so why did he feel as if she were pointing a finger at him?

Maybe his own self-conscious feelings were doing the pointing.

"You are, aren't you?" She leaned toward him, resting her elbow on the arm of the lawn chair. Her voice was whispery as she continued, "You were trying to gain his attention."

Pierce felt as if his face was a bull's-eye and she'd just jabbed him square in the nose.

He didn't have to confirm her suspicion. She knew the truth for what it was without his having to utter a single word. Her dark eyes were shadowed with sincere empathy.

"Oh, Pierce, isn't it amazing?" She sighed. She reclined against the chair back. "The adults from our childhood have such an influence on each of us. The sisters had me vowing to get out of Lebo at any cost in order to see the world they presented to me in books. And your dad influenced your career choice. And it's quite possible that none of them even knew how they were affecting us." Her head wobbled slowly from side to side. "I don't believe the nuns realized a thing."

"My father never suspected how he influenced me." Again he marveled at how easy it was to confess his secrets to Amy. How easy it was to express his feelings. "He took no notice of my intellectual interests."

The sympathy she felt deepened significantly. Her compassion warmed the air between them.

"It's so upsetting to hear the anger in your voice," she told him. "Are you so sure your father wasn't interested? Could it be that he was busy trying to make a living? To provide you and your sister and your mother with all that he could?"

"Oh, he was a great provider, all right. He provided for himself. For his work. He built the original lab. The original greenhouse. But the home he provided for his family was a disgrace. My mother slept in a bedroom that was ten feet square for the full duration of her marriage. My father had a bankful of money, yet he couldn't part with a penny to give her a home she could be proud of. Hell, he couldn't see clear to fix the damned leaky roof. He didn't care, Amy. He just didn't care about us."

Dark emotions swirled in his gut. He'd made a mistake in opening this can of worms. But there was something about this beautiful woman sitting next to him under the great white oak...something that loosened a man's lips. Lowered his guard.

"What bothers me more than anything," he continued, "was that I actually tried to cultivate a relationship with him."

"You did?"

"I studied his work. Planned my entire education around his ideas, his ambitions. And just when I'd earned my doctorate, just when I was ready to return home and join my father's business, what did he do?"

She studied him pensively.

"He suffered a stroke in the lab. He died, Amy. He died and made it impossible for me to ever—" The rest of his thought refused to come as bleak emotions bombarded him, fusing into an ugly conglomeration that overwhelmed him.

Her fingertips slid over his forearm, like warm silk gliding lusciously across his flesh.

"I'm sorry, Pierce."

He basked in the nearness of her, the solace of her presence. He sighed, his shoulders rounding as his tension eased. He hadn't realized how uptight he'd become.

She gave his arm a gentle squeeze. "I'm just so sorry. I hate the thought that you spent so many years studying and you end up unhappy with your choice of—"

"No, no," he interrupted. "I'm not unhappy with my career. I love my work. I've always been fascinated with biology. With nature sciences. Plant genetics. It's just that…well, that…" Confusion had him pausing.

"If you're satisfied with the way your life turned out," she murmured, "then I'm afraid I don't quite understand why you're so angry with your father."

"Oh, Amy, I apologize. I never meant to dump this complicated mess on you."

"It's okay. Dump away."

Her small smile was encouraging, and he offered her one in return.

Trolling through his memories, he paused a moment. Making her understand the situation—his mind-set—all those years ago seemed terribly important.

"I was always," he began tentatively, "very troubled by my father's indifference."

She winced, but he knew the description fit in every sense of the word.

"As a kid, I couldn't help wondering if there was something wrong with me. Some reason that he might feel embarrassed by me. But that conclusion didn't last long. You see, my father was just as indifferent to my sister and my mother. His work was all that ever mattered to him."

He inhaled deeply, then released the sigh with force. "I decided that the only way I'd ever reach him was to force him to relate to me. To make him sit up and take notice."

Chagrin sent heat suffusing his face and neck. When he heard his past verbalized, it made him come off looking...desperate.

"And you did that," Amy supplied, "by becoming an expert in his field."

"Why does it sound so wretchedly pathetic?"

"Pierce, there's nothing wrong with your wanting to connect with your father. Absolutely nothing."

"Well, those years of keeping my nose to the academic grindstone were all for nothing," he said. "The moment I was ready to join forces with him— to formulate some kind of relationship with him—he up and died on me."

"Don't say it was for nothing. There are so many people in this world who would love the chance t-to—" her voice hitched "—to educate themselves as you have."

Something snapped and sparked, causing his very skin to bristle. Amy's passion suddenly consumed her.

"You said you like what you do," she pointed out.

"I love what I do."

"So it wasn't for nothing. It *wasn't*."

He nodded. His larynx felt swollen and sore as he admitted, "You're right." When he swallowed, his throat undulated jerkily as suppressed emotion gathered there.

She studied his face. Finally she said, "Could it be, Pierce, that you're not really angry with your dad? That you're more, well, sad that things didn't turn out between the two of you as you'd planned?"

Glancing down at where her hand still rested on his arm, he studied her smooth skin, the tiny hills of her knuckles, the tapered length of her fingers.

Without looking up, he said, "I am sad. I feel as if something in me is missing. A hole, that can never be filled. But I'm angry, too, Amy. I'm damned livid." He lifted his gaze to her. "My father had the ability to fill that hole. But he chose not to."

Moisture glistened in her beautiful brown eyes, and she tightened her grip in silent support. She didn't speak. Sometimes words simply weren't necessary.

They sat in the sunshine and watched the boys galloping on imaginary horses around the ragtag castle they had built.

New emotions mingled with the dark ones tumbling inside him. He felt encouraged. Validated. But most of all he felt shored up by Amy. By her compassion and her understanding.

Yes, there was something about this woman, Pierce decided. Something spectacular.

Chapter Eight

Amy came down the stairs after having settled the boys into bed. They'd had a long, full day. She was looking forward to an hour or so of quiet before she called it a night herself.

She entered the kitchen and stopped dead.

Pierce stood by the table, his face tight.

"What is it? What's wrong?"

"This arrived at the lab late this afternoon by courier." He held up a sheet of paper. "It's a letter from the perfumery, and someone neglected to have it translated for me."

He was upset. She didn't have to ask if this was a problem for him.

"They know full well that—" he lifted his free hand, palm up "—I don't speak French."

Hoping to lighten his mood, she quipped, "The important question is, do you *read* French?"

The tension reflected in his green eyes eased and

he smiled. "That is the important question. And the answer is no. I neither speak nor read French."

"As your nephews might say, that sure sucks for you."

"Amy!" Mirth laced his admonishment, clear proof that her audacity both shocked and amused him. "We've scolded the boys for using that word."

Her naughtiness had them both laughing.

"Just how big is this bump in the road?" she asked after a moment.

"Not a huge one. The routine has been that I'm sent an English translation of all correspondence. Guess this one just got by them. I'm sure someone from the head office can fax a translation to me, but I couldn't get an answer when I called. They've evidently gone home for the day, so it'll have to wait until tomorrow." He shrugged. "I am curious about the contents of the letter, though. I've been waiting for some word from them about the flower scent I've been working on."

"I might be able to help."

He brightened. "You think?"

"My French is nowhere near fluent, but I'll be happy to give it a try. Let me go get my French dictionary. That should help." She turned toward the stairs to her room.

"Meet me in the study," he called after her.

When she returned with dictionary in hand, Pierce had poured out two glasses of wine. He picked up one glass by its stem and offered it to her.

"I thought we could use a drink while we translate."

"Thank you." She took a sip. Then she caught his

gaze over the rim of the delicate glass, the omnipresent hum that vibrated between them making itself known in a very big way. She swallowed.

"Should we get started?" Without waiting for an answer, Amy set the book and the wine on the desktop and looked down at the letter. She studied it for a moment and then placed her finger on the header. "It is from the perfume company—" she grinned up at him "—but you already knew that much."

"Jean Langfitt is the man with whom I have the most contact."

The proper grammar he used would have sounded stilted had she been the one who used it. Suddenly she felt lacking. How on earth could someone like her help someone like him?

He doesn't know you're deficient, a quiet voice reminded her.

She found the man's name at the bottom of the paper. "Yes, it's from Dr. Langfitt. Did you know that Jean is the French version of John?"

"I didn't," he said.

"And Dr. Langfitt is the company's director of…um—"

"Research and development," he supplied. He pulled the desk chair out for her. "Sit. I don't want you hunching over. Who knows how long this will take?" Then he slid a side chair over next to her and sat down beside her.

Amy was cognizant of the fact that his knee was pressed against her thigh, but she tried her darnedest to ignore it *and* the electric surges his nearness sent skittering across her skin.

"Okay." She focused every ounce of concentration

on the paper in front of her. "Let's see. He hopes you are well—that sentence was easy enough. *'Je suis heureux de vous faire part que le parfum extrait de vos fleurs a fait frémir notre nez.'*" She murmured to herself, "*Fait fémir* is thrilled. *Fleurs* is flowers. So this guy is pleased to report…" She shook her head as her voice trailed off. "This doesn't make sense, Pierce."

She flipped through the dictionary. And after only a couple of minutes rechecking the translation, she began, "From this letter…" Confusion had her shaking her head and the rest of her sentence trailed off. "But that would be a silly thing for him to say…." Again she stopped, feeling embarrassed that she might not be able to help him after all.

All she could do was give the translation her best shot.

"According to this," she said, pointing to a line of the letter, "Dr. Langfitt's nose is thrilled with the scents extracted from your flowers."

Immediately it became obvious that Pierce understood the strange statement.

His mouth widened in a relieved grin. "Not nose as in the body part. *Nose*. With a capital *N*."

She still didn't get it, and she was sure her face expressed just that.

"A Nose," he explained, "is the job title of the person who mixes scents. The person who creates the different perfumes sold around the world."

His green eyes twinkled with excitement, and it was impossible not to get caught up in it. But she dipped her chin and directed her gaze back to the letter.

"Well," she continued, "according to the good doctor—" she reached for her dictionary again "—the Nose wasn't able to reproduce, no, duplicate...the Nose wasn't able to duplicate the scent of your flower."

"Woo-hoo!" Pierce lifted his fist into the air, joy exploding from him like air from a balloon that had been poked with a pin.

She started, and couldn't help but laugh along with him. This was obviously very good news.

"You see, if the scent of the flower I created could be duplicated by mixing already known fragrances," he explained, "my work would have been worthless."

The joy rushing through him made his already handsome face even more so. Amy couldn't help but stare.

"There are different types of fragrances," he continued, evidently unaware of the rude manner in which she gaped. "Woodsy scents like cedar and sandalwood. Animal scents, mostly musk. Flower essences. There are thousands of those. Fruit extracts and oils. What makes my flower special is that its fragrance combines an intriguing combination that subtly mimics aspects of them all."

"Amazing." Taking her eyes off his gorgeous face, his animated features, was impossible.

"My best selling point was my belief that the scent from my flower can be used in perfumes for both men and women."

Calling herself captivated wouldn't have been far off the mark. "So...this *is* good news."

"This isn't just good news. This is *great* news. My

hybrid flower has a natural fragrance that can't be duplicated by an expert. This means a patent. And more money than I'll be able to spend in my lifetime.''

She thought about the custom-built home he lived in, his huge piece of property, the lab, the greenhouse. He already had everything he could possibly want.

''Something tells me,'' she surmised, the words tumbling off her tongue before she thought much about it, ''that your happiness doesn't rely much on money.''

He sighed. ''You're right. It has very little to do with money.''

''You're pleased because you've done something remarkable.''

Pierce only smiled.

Because she thought he needed to hear the words, she whispered, ''Your father would be proud.''

Time seemed to hover, and for the span of a single heartbeat Amy feared he had been offended. But then he reached up and cupped her cheek in the palm of his hand.

''I could just kiss you.''

She couldn't draw breath. And it was almost a certainty that she was going to fall into the intense depths of his eyes.

''I think I will.''

He leaned in and covered her mouth with his. The red merlot on his lips, on his tongue tasted heady, and although Amy had barely tasted the wine in her glass, she felt drunk. Inebriated beyond reason.

She closed her eyes, took his bottom lip between her teeth and nibbled. Without breaking contact with his mouth, she smiled when she heard the low groan that rumbled deep in his throat.

Warning flags began waving furiously in her head. This wasn't right! This was the very thing she'd been working so hard to avoid.

She whispered his name and knew that all she was feeling was expressed in her tone.

"Please—" His voice was as rusty as old nails. "Let's just enjoy this moment, Amy. Just this one moment. No strings attached. Just…let me…"

He kissed her, and if Amy had felt intoxicated a moment before, it was nothing compared to the wooziness infecting her now. Her knees quivered even though she was seated. The muscles of her arms quaked with weakness. Even her spine seemed to have become fragile and frail, and she was sure she would slide right out of the chair onto the floor.

But she didn't. What she did do was surrender to Pierce's plea. And she savored every second.

Oh, boy, did she ever!

She lowered her lids, leaned into him and slid her hands along his corded forearms, the fine, springy hairs tickling the sensitive skin between her fingers. Where flesh contacted flesh, Amy felt scorched by the velvet heat of him.

And he kissed her.

Barraged with sensation, she moved her palms upward, felt his tight biceps, his broad shoulders, the expanse of his chest beneath the soft cotton of his shirt.

And he kissed her.

His hands cradled her face, their tongues dancing erotically. The scent of him swirled around her, filling her nostrils. The feel of his pounding heart thundered beneath her fingertips. The wine-sweet taste of him pervaded her very existence.

And he kissed her.

Desire slugged through her body, engorging her, inflaming her to heights she'd never before imagined. She wanted him close, and, as if of their own volition, her hands clenched the front of his shirt and tugged him to her.

And he kissed her.

Through the sensual haze fogging her brain she became cognizant that his hand had dropped from her face to cup her breast. Her nipple tightened into a hard and lusciously painful nub when he lightly grazed the pad of his thumb over it.

He pulled his mouth from hers, but kept his lips so close that she could feel each gasping breath he took. With a touch that was feather soft, he roved his full bottom lip down over the curve of her chin. His moist mouth rambled a path of sweet kisses up her jaw, over her cheek and temple. His lips swept across her forehead like the echo of a whisper, then they made their way oh-so-slowly, oh-so-lightly down the bridge of her nose.

The kiss had ended. But the moments of bone-deep passion hadn't lessened one iota. In fact, the fervor pumping through her rose to a fever pitch.

Her body felt racked as she struggled to inhale oxygen into her lungs. He was so close, and she yearned so deeply, that she came to the conclusion that there was only one aim for them. One end.

To become one. To bond in the most intimate way a man and woman could.

The thought made her eyes fly open, and she saw that he was staring at her. His gaze was drugged with his overwhelming need. Never in her life had she felt more feminine, more desired.

"Amy, we've got to stop. I know I said we should enjoy the moment, but…honey—" his swallow was jerky "—we've got to stop before this goes too far."

She knew he was right. Well, her head knew he was. But her heart and her body wanted to scream, *"Why?"*

Not too much later they sat in the living room, he on the couch and she in a chair. However, even though they took great care to keep their distance, Amy could feel that something had changed between them. Something incredible. On several different levels.

Like a volcano that had unleashed itself in an explosion of molten lava, the force of their burning attraction had diminished. Oh, it was still there. Continued to simmer. But the kiss they'd shared had acted as a relief valve of sorts that had released the pressure they'd both suffered.

And Amy couldn't help but conclude that the very core of their relationship had been transformed, as well. She felt comfortable with him. She trusted him with every fiber of her being.

The fact that he'd been as charged with passion as she, yet had possessed the strength and the willpower to end the kiss was proof that he was worthy of her trust. He knew that getting involved wasn't what she wanted. He knew she wouldn't have wanted to cross the line. And he'd kept that from happening. He'd kept his cool.

He had let her know by his actions that he could be relied upon, could be counted on to do the right thing…no matter how heated the situation might become. That meant a great deal to Amy.

She found her heart was warm and pliant. What she was feeling was gratitude. He could have taken her tonight. She'd have gladly given the very essence of herself to him. However, he'd made certain that that hadn't happened. The appreciation gathering in her chest had her wanting to do something nice for him. Made her want to give him a gift to replace that most precious one he could so easily have acquired, but had chosen to respectfully decline.

"Isn't it incredible," she finally said, "how we are shaped by our past?"

"I know I sure was." Pierce leaned forward and refilled her glass with the merlot.

The small smile she offered him conveyed her silent thanks.

"But it's also incredible," Amy continued, "how the past shapes each of us differently."

A tiny frown creased the area between his eyebrows and she could tell he wasn't certain what she meant.

She explained, "Take you and your sister, for instance. You were raised by the same mother, had the same father, suffered the same paternal neglect, yet each of you grew up with greatly differing opinions regarding love and family and relationships."

The pucker remained embedded in his brow.

"Oh, come on now." She chuckled. "Don't tell

me you haven't ever thought your sister's choice of husbands was…a little different from the norm." Reaching out, she picked up her wineglass from where it sat on the coffee table.

"I'm not that much younger than your sister," she told Pierce. "When Cynthia came to Lebo with Reverend Winthrop, I was aware of the talk." A grin spread over her mouth. "You know how small-town people can be. Gossip becomes a recreation."

His features relaxed, then he actually smiled. Delight seeped through her like liquid fire, warm and enticing.

"People whispered about—" she lowered her voice to a bare hush "—the age difference."

Pierce laughed outright.

"They certainly didn't mean any harm, you know," Amy continued. "It just gave them something to talk about. Some way to pass the time." She paused long enough to take a sip from her glass. The wine tasted luscious, the flavor reminding her of the heady tang of Pierce's kiss.

She blinked, moistened her lips and *focused*.

"Even the least talented armchair psychologist would be led to the conclusion that your sister just might have been looking for a father figure."

He looked thoughtful now, his gaze suddenly weighty with reflection.

"I admit," he said, "that I had the same thought when Cynthia announced her plans to marry John."

"However, your father had a most dramatically opposite effect on your attitudes regarding family."

Pierce nodded.

She'd laid the groundwork. Now was the time for

her to lay her tiny pearl of wisdom on that foundation…offer him a small but terribly important gift.

"You've claimed," she began, "that you're just like your father. That you're so caught up in your work that you could never be good daddy material." She paused in order to make an impression. Then she added, "But I wonder if you've allowed yourself to be, well, deluded."

His pensive expression tightened. He was frowning again. But Amy was determined to bestow her thoughts on him—a notion that just might free him from the prison in which he'd interned himself.

When she didn't immediately clarify her statement, he said, "Deluded? How so?"

"I don't believe you're anything like your father."

Her bold proclamation made the pucker between his eyebrows deepen.

She scrunched up her nose. "Let me rephrase that. I believe you're less like your father than you perceive."

His glass sat on the end table, forgotten, as he concentrated every nuance of his attention on her. His gem-green eyes darkened with wariness, but she resisted the urge to look away.

She pressed forward with resolve. "Yes, like your father, you love your work. And your choice of careers is right along the lines of his. And I believe that there was a time when you spent every waking moment in your lab and the greenhouse. That you were truly absorbed with your research, your experiments. I believe that if you wanted to, you could become an honest-to-goodness workaholic. Just like your father."

Leaning forward, she set her glass on the table. She continued in a whisper-soft tone, "But Pierce, you have to admit that all that changed once your nephews came to stay with you."

His eyes, his expression, his thoughts were indecipherable. She hadn't a clue what was going on in his head, or what he might be feeling about what she said. At any moment he could explode in anger, or hug her with gratitude—she couldn't tell.

"Your behavior toward those boys," she told him, pointing toward the ceiling, toward that part of the house where Benjamin and Jeremiah were fast asleep, "has been filled with nothing but love and kindness and concern. You care about those children. That much is obvious. And you've given generously of your time." Emotion tightened her throat and she had to strain to continue. "Something your own father never did."

His jaw tensed and his eyes glistened. The sigh he heaved was heavy.

"But Amy—" his voice nearly broke "—anyone can do something, act a certain way, for a short time. A few weeks. A month or two. But old habits die hard—"

"But they *can* die."

He looked unconvinced.

After a moment he reached up and scrubbed his fingertips back and forth across his forehead. "I appreciate what you're trying to do here. But I just can't agree with you. Haven't you ever heard that old adage that the fruit doesn't fall far from the tree?"

Astonishment widened her eyes. "How can you say that? What about Cynthia? The two of you grew up in the same house. Under the same circumstances.''

He rested his elbow on the arm of the couch. ''Why is this so important all of a sudden? I've survived just fine being on my own—''

''That's why it's so important, Pierce,'' she said, slicing his sentence clean in two. ''You haven't survived just fine.''

His whole body seemed to grow taut. Clearly he wasn't happy with her estimation. If she was reading his features correctly, he found her belief to be something akin to a wild accusation.

Before he could become too aggravated with her, she rushed to explain. ''What I mean is, it seems to me that your life here…before the boys arrived…has been, well, kind of lonely. You spend your time with your plants, doing your research. You're too isolated, Pierce. Too secluded. It isn't natural. It isn't right.''

''Wait a minute now.'' He bristled. ''It's not like I'm a hermit. I've dated. Cynthia has pushed quite a few women on me over the years.''

She cast him a sardonic expression. ''A few dates here and there, with women who are pushed on you. What kind of life is that?''

''My life is right for me, Amy. In fact, it's perfect for me.''

Oh, Lord, she had made him angry. That hadn't been her intention at all.

''Please, Pierce, just listen to me. I'm not suggesting this to annoy you. I only want you to be happy. And I've seen you with Benjamin and Jeremiah. You love those kids.''

Agitation caused a tiny muscle near his temple to twitch. His eyes narrowed.

"Of course I love those boys. They're my sister's children. They're precious. A blessing in my life. But that doesn't mean that I should go out and get married and raise children of my own. I'm not cut out to be a father."

The words seemed to slice and cut at him as he voiced them. He didn't like the situation he found himself in, that was clear to Amy, even if he hadn't recognized it.

"You have to trust me on this."

Those words reminded her of how much she did trust him now, and how that trust had been cultivated. Heat flooded her, filling her with thankfulness. She would make him understand. Even if she had to spend the whole night explaining it to him.

"And *you* have to trust *me*," she gently insisted.

At that, the anger seemed to drain from him. He reclined against the cushioned back of the couch and simply waited for her to expound. She had no intention of disappointing him.

"You told me that your father never spent time with you. That he never gave you the attention he should have. That he never attended a single ball game." She let her tongue skitter across her lips. "Well, I've seen you playing ball with your nephews. Swimming with them. Racing around the yard with them. Making up silly games with them. And you *enjoyed* it.

"If you had that much fun with Benjamin and Jeremiah, how much more would you enjoy spending time with your own children?"

Evidently the question made him uncomfortable, for he trained his eyes on the far side of the room.

"Pierce."

She stopped, determined that he would look at her as she spoke. What she had to tell him was that important, in her opinion. Only when his gaze was once again leveled on hers did she continue.

"You *made* time for those boys—and continue to make time. You talk to them. More important, you listen to them. You let them know that they're loved. That they're appreciated. And you do all those things not because you have to, but because you want to. It's what you feel. It's what you know they need. Just think how magnified all of this would be if you were their dad rather than their uncle."

He seemed to be holding his breath.

"I understand you're worried about your ability to sustain this kind of behavior," she quietly told him. "But I think the answer is simple. It's all about balance. A person balances their work life and their family life. You're doing a wonderful job of that with Benjamin and Jeremiah. And I think it would be very easy for you to maintain it…were you to have a family of your own."

Silence fell between them like a light dusting of fine sand.

He toyed with his chin between his thumb and index finger. Finally he lowered his hand into his lap.

"I don't know what to say."

Amy smiled. "Don't say anything. All I ask is that you think about what I've said." She sighed, feeling suddenly exhausted. "Just…think."

And that's exactly what he was doing. However, that was exactly what she was doing, too.

Would he even perceive her as someone he wanted to listen to?

Perception was everything. Hadn't she learned that lesson all too well?

He didn't know who or what she was. He didn't know the truth. He respected her. He saw her as competent. Knowledgeable. Hadn't he said as much? She'd fooled him well.

And because she had done such a thorough job of it, he would take note of all she'd said. He would heed her advice. And who knew? The gift she'd given him tonight might very well change his thinking…his view of himself…his opinion of love and family.

What she'd said—her gift—might very well change his whole life.

Chapter Nine

Pierce studied the final flat of plants, carefully recording in the data book the number of buds on each stem. Just as he'd hypothesized, the quantity of buds had doubled with this group of plantings. The flowers in this flat of plants were within days of blooming. The lab would fill once again with that very special fragrance that couldn't be duplicated, even by the best perfume experts in Provence.

His grin went wide at the thought and he reclined in the chair. His experiments were working, and the method he'd developed to get to this point would make him a wealthy man.

Your father would be proud. Those words scuttled through his thoughts like scampering mice.

Maybe his father would be proud, Pierce thought. But what mattered to him even more, he realized, was the satisfaction of knowing he was making a name for himself in the world of plant science. Contentment warmed him and he basked in this feeling of accomplishment.

The news that he'd actually invented a flower with a unique aroma had made him ecstatic. The fact that Amy had been the person to deliver the news via her halting French had made the moment extra special.

He closed the data book, tucked his pen neatly into his shirt pocket and then returned the plants to the environmentally controlled chamber with the other foliage in varying stages of growth.

The kiss he and Amy had shared three nights ago had shaken him to the very core. Passion had ensnared them both in its hot grip. He'd surmised that both of them could easily have lost complete control.

However, his respect for Amy—for the life goals that were all-important to her—had won out in the end, and he'd resisted the spell that had so thoroughly swept them up.

But, oh, what succulent moments those had been. Holding her, touching her, tasting her. The experience had been one he would never forget.

Continuing to savor those memories, he spent a few minutes clearing off his desktop. The smile was still on his mouth when he flipped off the lights in the laboratory, locked the door and started across the yard toward the house.

Fluffy clouds floated in a sky that was an amazing azure-blue, and Pierce slowed his steps in order to appreciate the sight. The water of the bay reflected the sun's rays, sparkling like a million diamond chips on a backdrop of blue-green velvet.

He wondered what the boys had been up to today. What stories would they have to share over dinner?

Then he thought of Amy's beautiful face, and his smile hitched a notch.

Pierce's steps came to a complete halt as he became cognizant of his behavior. He had ended his workday while the sun was still well above the horizon. He'd unconsciously straightened up his work space and locked up his lab in time to have dinner with his nephews and Amy.

And he'd been doing it for quite a while now.

You're less like your father than you perceive.

Amy had pulled no punches with him when she'd made the proclamation. She'd made quite an argument to back up the statement, as well. She'd pointed out that he'd enjoyed spending time with Benjamin and Jeremiah.

The hint of accusation in her tone when she'd spoken those words had him chuckling under his breath, even now.

She'd been absolutely right, of course. Interacting with the boys continued to be a pure delight for him. In the past, he'd seen Benjamin and Jeremiah when he'd had dinner with his sister and her family about once a month, or on birthdays and holidays. But with the children living under his roof, he had enjoyed a true taste of what it might be like to have a family of his own.

As Amy had suggested, if he loved his nephews enough to inadvertently change his work schedule in order to be with them, how much more would he be willing to do for children of his own?

He stood on the grass, staring out at the Delaware Bay, dumbfounded as he realized that his comparison between himself and his father was collapsing like a sand castle at high tide.

Amy's calm and compassionate gaze swam in his head. He wanted to see her, couldn't wait to tell her that he now believed she'd been right. He *was* less like his father than he'd imagined himself to be.

Benjamin and Jeremiah's stay had helped him to understand that. However, he was wise enough to realize that the boys hadn't been the only reason for his coming to this conclusion.

Smoothing his hand across the back of his neck, Pierce couldn't help but admit that Amy, and his desire to be with her, had somehow been an even bigger motivating factor in this surprising revelation.

His gaze was on her again, Amy didn't have to look across the dinner table to know it. She felt it. The heat of his stare was as intense as a laser beam.

For the past few days the air between them had been light and breezy. Fun. They had laughed and talked together, had indulged themselves in this new and easy camaraderie. However, something had happened to him. Something had changed. She'd sensed it the very second he'd walked through the door late this afternoon.

His handsome face had been taut, his gaze containing something powerful yet inscrutable. At first she'd thought he was having some kind of problem in the lab. But she'd asked him how his day had gone and he'd told her all was fine with his work.

The manner in which he'd focused that formidable energy on her led her to the quick realization that whatever had happened to him in some way involved her.

Attempting to act as normally as possible, she'd rummaged around the kitchen, slicing the pork loin, dishing up the vegetables and setting the table. Finally she'd called the boys to eat. But as the meal progressed, she'd caught the distinct impression that the pressure beneath the crust of that all-too-passionate volcano they'd experienced just a few evenings ago was once again building, and that frightened the devil out of her.

She had barely survived the erotic moments she'd spent in Pierce's arms the night she had translated the letter for him. His kiss had erased all of her inhibitions, had obliterated every vestige of her self-control. She'd forgotten all about her dreams and desires.

No, she decided, those sensuous moments had nothing whatsoever to do with her *forgetting* her desires. Those had been ignited by the mere nearness of him.

Had Pierce not severed contact between them, had he not saved her by pulling away from her, who knew where they might have ended up. In bed? Or would her need have caused her to surrender herself right there on the plush carpet in his study?

Heat rushed to her cheeks like tiny twin blazes at the thought.

"What are you guys doing tonight?"

She looked over at Jeremiah, puzzled by the wording of his question. "Us guys?"

The boy nodded, picking up a green bean with his fingers.

"Use your fork," she gently scolded him.

He picked up the utensil and speared the bean. It hovered near his mouth as he said, "I meant you and Uncle Pierce."

Amy's gaze moved to Pierce, and his minute shrug told her he was as bewildered as she.

"We're going to spend the evening with you," Pierce said, looking from one of his nephews to the other. "Isn't that the normal routine?"

That's when Benjamin spoke up. "Me and Jeremiah were talkin' today. And we have an awesome idea."

As jittery as Pierce had made Amy, she was helpless against the grin that crept over her lips. Young Benjamin looked like a tiny version of an experienced attorney who was about to announce some great bombshell that would clinch a hard-fought defense case.

"We realized," Benjamin continued, "that we haven't had a kids' night since Mommy and Daddy left."

"A kids' night?" Pierce absently wiped the tips of his fingers on his linen napkin.

Jeremiah nodded, but was too busy chewing to explain. His brother eagerly piped up. "Kids' night is when the kids get to take over the TV. We bring our sleeping bags down from upstairs. We pick out three or four of our favorite movies—"

"Three or four movies?" Amy tried to keep the disapproval from her voice, but she was sure she'd failed. "Why, that means you'll be up—"

"Really late!" Jeremiah supplied, his round gaze conveying his excitement over the prospect.

Benjamin wasn't the least put off by her interruption. "Yeah, and we get to have lots of stuff to eat. Chips. Pretzels. Nachos. Soda."

"And popcorn," his brother added.

Amy didn't like the sound of this at all. "But you've just had dinner."

Jeremiah groaned. "Amy, kids' night just wouldn't be the same without junk food."

She looked across the table at Pierce, hoping for some support with this outrageous suggestion. Her imagination ran rampant with thoughts of bellyaches in the night and grumpy children in the morning. However, Pierce's attention was firmly on the boys.

"What are Amy and I supposed to do for the evening?" he queried.

The twins offered him identical shrugs.

"You could play cards," Jeremiah suggested. "Or you could borrow our new jigsaw puzzle."

Benjamin reached for his milk. "Mommy and Daddy never had a problem finding some way to keep busy in their room."

That's when Pierce chose to lift his gaze to her face, his eyes sparking with a naughty light. "I'm sure they didn't," he said, his voice low, bordering on sultry.

Giddiness tickled Amy's stomach.

Without hesitation Benjamin added, "They were pretty good at keeping out of our way on kids' night." He swiped at his mouth with the back of his hand. "I think they played board games up in their bedroom."

Impishness shone in Pierce's green gaze as he stared at her from across the table.

She slid her chair back and stood up. "Pierce,

could I see you in the kitchen a minute? You can help me carry in the apple pie.''

"But I'm not finished with dinner yet,'' Jeremiah said. "This is good, so don't rush me.''

She chuckled. "Well, thank you for the nice compliment. We'll be right back. You just continue enjoying your dinner. You, too, Benjamin, okay?''

The boys nodded and tucked in. Pierce set his napkin beside his dinner plate and followed her from the room.

"Can you believe my sister?'' he asked as they entered the kitchen. "She wants a little whoopee time with her husband and she cons her children into believing they're getting some great deal with a night of videos and junk food. She even christens the event with a special name.'' He snickered. "Kids' night, indeed. Just wait until Cynthia gets home. I am going to tease her something fierce.''

Amy closed the refrigerator door and set the pie on the countertop.

"Pierce, I'm not so sure the boys should be staying up until all hours of the night.''

"Oh, what can it hurt?''

"But they have a bedtime,'' she pointed out. "You know that. And we've both been very strict with them about following it.''

He lifted one shoulder. "From what the boys were saying in there, their own parents aren't all that strict about bedtime. Not on kids' night, anyway.'' Suddenly he couldn't contain his mirth. "In fact, sounds to me as if my sister lets her children have the run of the house anytime she and John want to—'' he waggled his eyebrows "—you know what.''

Heat tinged her cheeks pink. She turned to the cabinet and took down dessert plates. When she twisted around, Pierce was so close that he startled her. He took the plates from her, his fingers brushing hers.

"Honestly, Amy," he said, "I can't see why the boys shouldn't have a special night."

"But chips and pretzels and nachos? All that junk is enough to choke a horse. They'll be sick."

"Don't forget the popcorn."

"I'm serious here."

He smiled as he set the plates on the counter next to the pie. "I'm serious, too. They'll be just fine."

Although he hadn't moved an inch that she could tell, it felt as if he'd drawn closer to her. The air between them became dense, sultry.

"Like you said, they're used to going to bed early."

Although he was sticking to the topic, Amy sensed that his mood was shifting back into the sensual mode she couldn't help but notice when he'd stared at her across the dinner table just a moment or two ago.

"They'll be asleep before the second movie is half over."

She sighed in an attempt to hide the jitteriness that had suddenly developed low in her belly. "Okay. I guess it'll be all right."

The smile that raided his sexy lips was languorous, lingering, and the shiver that coursed down her spine at the sight of it made her want to arch her back. Instead she crossed her arms over her chest and grasped her forearms firmly.

Her body language shouted at him to move away, to give her some space.

It seemed, however, that he was playing deaf to her silent messages.

He edged toward her. Not much. Just a fraction of an inch. But it was enough to cause her chest to grow tight. She went all woozy.

"The real question is," he whispered, "what are you and I going to do to keep ourselves busy?"

His mouth looked so inviting. And those green eyes of his had never appeared more enticing than they did right now...darkened by yearning.

For her.

He lifted his hand, ran his fingertips down the length of her jaw, his touch as light as a sigh.

A fit of nervousness had her throat undulating with a swallow.

"Pierce."

She had hoped to put warning in her tone, but all she heard was a single, singsong note that was so muted she worried that he wouldn't even be aware that she'd spoken.

"Oh," he crooned, "I know we're not supposed to be doing this." He tugged at her earlobe and murmured, "Why is it that forbidden fruit is always the sweetest?"

Her fortitude began to dissolve, like chips of ice on a hot summer's day. And when he traced the outer rim of her ear with the pad of his finger, she closed her eyes and focused every nuance of her attention on keeping her legs from buckling beneath her.

She raised her lids and lifted her gaze to his, her heart pounding, her blood slogging through her veins.

"Tell me—" He was so close, she felt his warm

breath against her cheek as he spoke. "Have you ever had anything more luscious than forbidden fruit?"

Her breath left her in a sigh, and she thought she'd faint dead away from the weight of the wanton carnality that washed through her body.

As if trapped in a hazy dream, she released her shielding hold on her forearms and splayed her palms on his chest. Then she lifted her face, rose on her toes and captured his mouth with hers.

In that very instant, Amy learned something astounding.

There really was nothing in the entire universe that tasted as sweet as the forbidden fruit that was his kiss.

When she pulled away from him, their lips parted with a soft, wet smack that made her grin. The scent of him floated around her like a sheer veil. The heat emanating from the solid mass of him made her feel cozy.

But then she blinked, and the fogginess that had warped her thinking began to clear. Her inhalation was shaky. She knew that the passion that had confined her had made her weak; however, she was also shocked that she hadn't fought it harder.

Attempting to step back, she felt the handle of the refrigerator door press into her back. She edged her face from him.

"Pierce—"

"I know, I know."

Something in his voice had her lifting her gaze to his. Emotion swam in his eyes. Remnants of need, disbelief, even remorse.

She took another breath, this one deeper, stronger. He said, "I know we weren't supposed to let that happen.'' He cleared his throat. The chuckle he emitted didn't seem to hold any humor, and the tension in his handsome face didn't ease. ''I guess I should apologize. Although, if I did, it wouldn't be all that sincere. But I think you're well aware of that.''

She searched his gaze, uncertain of what he expected her to say to that remark.

''So I think the thing to do—'' he picked up the dessert plates that he'd placed on the counter ''—is to try to act as if it hadn't happened at all.''

He turned then and walked away from her.

In the solitude of the kitchen she was bombarded by a mass of confusing emotions. Common sense was telling her he was right, yet at the same time her body and her heart were bellowing to be heard. She suspected—heck, she knew as surely as she knew her own name—that Pierce was experiencing the very same desires she was.

Just how long could the two of them continue to ignore these logic-crushing physical urges? And these irrational emotions?

The night was muggy; however, the wispy breeze blowing across the bay was just enough to allow Amy to enjoy the quiet. Translucent clouds scudded high overhead, diffusing the moonlight into a ghostly glow.

Okay, so she was hiding. At least she wasn't kidding herself. With the boys settled in their sleeping bags on the living-room floor, their favorite movies loaded into the DVD player, an abundance of snacks set about for their enjoyment, Amy had grown panicky about how she would spend the hours before her own bedtime.

Not wanting a repeat of the sweltering moments she'd spent with Pierce in the kitchen at dinner, she'd brought a paperback out to the shore and had settled on the grass to read. However, the spectacular sunset had been awe inspiring, and she'd set the book aside. The heavens had turned a thousand different shades of mauve before slowly growing inky.

And still she sat hugging her knees to her chest as she stared out across the black expanse of water.

The calmness in her spirit had been purposely instilled. Chaos hovered at the very edges of her consciousness, but she held it at bay.

How was she going to survive four more weeks under the same roof with Pierce when the attraction between them absolutely refused to go away? It also refused to be disregarded.

She'd survived this long, and she would endure her remaining weeks here with the boys. Here with Pierce. The thought had barely registered in her brain when doubt heaped itself onto her shoulders like shovels of hot coals.

Footsteps brushing though the thick grass behind her had her twisting toward the house.

"There you are." Pierce carried two tall glasses. "I brought you some iced tea," he told her. He stopped just a foot from where she sat. "Mind if I join you?"

She did mind.

"Of course not." To answer any other way would have gone against all the good manners her father had instilled in her.

He handed her one of the glasses and then squatted down onto the grass beside her. Condensation had formed on the outside of the tumbler, cold and wet against her fingers.

"It's hot out here."

Was that accusation she heard in his observation? Surely he was letting her know that he realized she was suffering the heat in order to hide from him.

But that was silly. How could he know? Hopefully, her self-consciousness had her imagining things.

Amy tried not to sound too defensive when she told him, "There's a breeze that kicks up every so often." Luckily, at that instant a light, humid waft of air swept across her cheek. "See? It's not all that bad."

She cast him a sidelong glance and saw that his mouth had twisted wryly. Tipping up her glass, she took a swallow. The cold, refreshing tea almost made her moan aloud.

"You've been hiding."

She nearly choked. Her whole body flamed with humiliation. He'd hit the nail right on the head. And worse yet, she'd been sitting out here feeling sticky and damp, all the while trying to convince herself it was a nice summer evening. Well, she didn't have to 'fess up entirely.

He turned his head toward her, his sexy green eyes demanding an answer.

A small groan issued from the back of her throat, then she confessed with a small, silent nod.

"There's no need, you know. I told you I'd ignore it."

She sat perfectly still.

Then he looked out at the horizon, where the soft

night met the inky sea. He muttered, "But it sure is determined not to be ignored."

She knew perfectly well what he said was true.

"In fact, it seems to be growing stronger with each passing day."

Hadn't she just come to that same conclusion herself?

Silence settled around them like the night.

Finally he nestled his glass of tea on the neatly trimmed lawn. "I've really enjoyed having you here. I think you know that." Potent emotion condensed his tone when he added, "I like you, Amy. A lot."

Panic had her heart puttering a staccato beat.

"You truly are an amazing woman. You're beautiful and—"

Skepticism elicited a most unladylike grunt from her that cut the rest of his thought short. She sensed that he teetered on the edge of being offended by her reaction.

"I'm serious. You're a striking woman, Amy. You thought that rouge and fancy face paint, those tailored clothes, were what made you enticing to me."

If the moment hadn't been so serious, she'd have smiled at his description of eye shadow and foundation, brow pencil and lipstick: the tools that helped her look professional.

"The attraction that I've felt for you," he continued, "only increased when you stopped wearing all that...stuff. We discovered that already. Talked about it, too."

She had hoped that her transformation would block the allure that vibrated between them. But she *had* quickly seen that she'd been sadly mistaken. He'd wanted her anyway.

And even though she'd fought it tooth and nail, the attraction she'd felt for him had never waned, but had grown and bloomed like a wild vine.

"You should know that the fascination I've found in you has much more substance to it than mere physical attraction. That part of the discovery we've never discussed. We haven't had the guts to talk about—to identify—what this thing between us really is."

Her spine straightened at his proclamation, every nerve on red alert. First, she couldn't believe he'd find her in the least fascinating, and second, he was telling her his emotions ran deeper than the physical level.

Unnerved by what he'd revealed, she pointed out, "But we shouldn't be talking about this. Not since we've decided to ignore it."

He frowned. "But I need you to know that you've taught me things about myself."

She felt her eyes widen, but she succeeded in suppressing the magnitude of her surprise.

"I believe you're right that I'm not so much like my father." He smoothed his fingers over his lower jaw. "I do love my work. It excites me and I thrive on it. But all the while that Benjamin and Jeremiah have been here my thoughts have kept turning to the boys at odd moments during the day. I wonder what they're doing. What they're getting into. What they're discovering. And I can't wait to see them each evening to hear all about their experiences. And I suspect that you were also correct when you said that I would only feel these things to a higher degree for children of my own."

His gaze latched onto hers. "I think about you, too, Amy. Throughout the day I—I wonder...I—" He pressed his lips together to cease his halting speech. His corded neck rippled in what was clearly a nervous swallow. "I can't wait to be with you each evening to hear all about your day." His tongue smoothed over his lips. "By dinnertime, the urge to leave the lab is so strong I just can't fight it. My father never experienced these kinds of amazing feelings for my mom or for my sister or for me. He couldn't have, you see, because if he had, he would never have been able to ignore them."

Warmth pumped through her body...through her soul. She liked the fact that she'd made him see he'd been mistaken about himself. She liked the fact that he now recognized he was kind and caring and concerned about his nephews. She also liked to hear that he wondered about her through his days in the lab, that he couldn't wait to see her each evening. She shouldn't like it, but she did.

"Amy, I know you've built some big dreams for yourself."

He paused long enough to inhale what she surmised was a bracing breath, the apprehension in it making her heart trip in her chest.

"But," he continued, "do you think there might be some way for us to explore—" he waved his hand back and forth in the space between them "—this?"

At that moment she felt as if he'd reached right into her chest and stolen her heart. The cavity behind her ribs was empty, yet she still lived and breathed. *Love truly was a miracle.*

She blanched as the realization hit her with mind-numbing force.

She loved him.

"We might be good together," he continued, his voice as soft as the bay breeze. "I have my work, of course. But there could be plenty of time for traveling. I go to Europe several times a year.

"You're a very smart woman, Amy. It's one of the reasons I feel so attracted to you. You're intelligent enough to figure out a way to…fit me into your future."

His choice of words sent her thoughts whirling into total chaos.

He toyed with the rim of the tumbler he'd set in the grass and she was grateful that this sudden bout of apparent timidity on his part diverted his attention. It gave her time to reign in her raucous reaction to what he'd said.

She *wasn't* a smart woman. No one had ever described her as such, and no one ever would. Everyone back in her hometown of Lebo had looked down on her because of her choices. The Oblate Sisters, especially, had voiced such disappointment in her. If Pierce knew the truth—she felt her blood freeze— he'd look down on her, too.

He lifted his gaze to hers. "We're both intelligent people. We ought to be able to work this out."

Panic bubbled up like thick green goo boiling over the rim of a caldron. It gathered in her throat, threatened to scorch her esophagus like hot acid. She bit back the raging turmoil with a jerky swallow, but she knew the look she leveled on him was stone-cold.

His green eyes shadowed with bewilderment, with hurt, even with a small flare of anger. "You're looking at me as if I just made the most loathsome suggestion you've ever heard."

Chapter Ten

Perception is everything.

Amy realized how proficient she'd become at pulling the wool over Pierce's eyes. He had no idea that she was none of the things he believed her to be. She'd succeeded in putting such a glorified slant on her story that Pierce would probably be blind to the honest truth even if she were to spell it all out for him in simple terms. Which she had no intention of doing. Ever. She couldn't begin to contemplate the humiliation of revealing her reality.

But now she was in deep trouble. The poor man was considering getting himself involved with a total fake. He needed to be saved from his own poor judgment.

Portraying herself as a woman who was smart and witty and capable for a couple of months was one thing. But she could never uphold that persona—continue to sustain the perception—forever. That would be an impossible task. For anyone, let alone a know-nothing from Nowhere, U.S.A.

''Pierce—''

When she heard the magnitude of emotion in her tone, she clamped her mouth shut. She must retain control of herself. But she had to admit she'd never felt such conflicting feelings in all her life.

Like warm honey, pure pleasure had rushed through her when she realized that he wanted her on more than just a physical level. She'd refused to even consider that what was between them was more complex than mere physical attraction, but he'd actually voiced it. And that had filled her with joy. However, her beautiful bliss hadn't been able to withstand the dread that had all too quickly bubbled up from deep inside her, gritty and thought-clogging as mud.

He perceived her forthcoming rejection—that much showed in his wounded gaze. Amy realized she'd revealed more when she'd spoken his name than she'd imagined. It grieved her to know she'd be hurting him, but as far as she could see it couldn't be helped. A small amount of time feeling rebuffed would be much better than making the mistake of his life.

That's what he'd be doing if she were to agree to what he was suggesting. By denying him, she'd be rescuing him. And he wasn't even aware of it.

Fire sparked in his eyes. His anguish manifested itself as anger. Good, she thought. Dealing with his ire would be easier than dealing with his hurt feelings.

''I can't believe you're going to reject the chance to explore what's between us, Amy.''

She'd love to delve into every vibe, every urge, every spark that flashed when the two of them were together. But she wouldn't put herself in a position of having it all only to lose it once he discovered the truth.

Facing the embarrassment of her past wasn't an option in her mind—she respected him too much, and wanted him to continue to respect her—so she'd have to lie as she'd never lied before. She didn't want to hurt him any more than she already had. But neither did she want to cope with the mortification that total honesty would bring.

"That's exactly what I'm going to do." She could feel the muscles in her body grow tight. "You know I have things I want to do. I'm not going to ruin all that for a few heated kisses."

"Is that all it meant to you?"

Disgust shadowed his handsome features like storm clouds, and she had to force herself not to flinch. Then she saw it again. Her words had hurt him, and Amy felt the icy vise of her concocted lies crushing her heart.

"I won't let you sit there and tell me that what we've felt—this thing that has ensnared us from the very beginning—is as frivolous as that."

She didn't dare respond. Not until she thoroughly thought through what she wanted to say, at least.

"I've learned things from you," he said. "Things I could never have learned from anyone else."

The breath she'd been holding left her body soundlessly. She could only stare.

"You made me see the truth about myself, Amy. You opened up my views. Made me rethink my plans for the future. Because of you, I've decided that I will make a good husband. A good and loving father."

You will! You will! But she didn't shout out that she agreed with him, didn't dare show the delight his change of heart gave her.

"Please don't tell me that this has been a one-way street," he said. "Please don't say that you haven't been touched, *changed,* by our time together these past weeks."

Annoyance tinged his tone, but she detected a heavy underpinning of entreaty.

"Of course I've—" Panic cut her confession to the quick. Resolve stiffened her spine. "Look, Pierce... does any of this really matter? I'm going to be leaving here—"

"Hell, yes, it matters!" Fiery anger flamed in his green eyes once more. "I refuse to believe I'm the only one who's been enlightened. You were adamant that you never wanted a husband, that you never wanted children. You only came here to care for my nephews because your father asked you to. Because you'd been grounded by the airlines. But I've seen you with Benjamin and Jeremiah. You've enjoyed yourself with them. More than you expected to. They've stirred something in you. I've witnessed it.

"And I refuse to let you deny that you have feelings for me. I saw the look in your eyes when I stroked your skin, Amy. When I kissed your lips, I felt your body come alive. When I touch you... something amazing happens."

She realized that her teeth were clenched tight. So were her fists. If she didn't put some space between them, she was going to crack like a delicate robin's egg. He would know all her secrets... and she'd be left with nothing more than his shock and his disdain.

Pressing her fingers against the ground, she sprang to her feet. Somewhere in the haze of her panic she felt her sandal come into contact with the nearby glass, heard the sound of ice and liquid spilling on the ground.

"I told you." She spit out the words. "I have plans for my life. I have goals and aspirations. I explained it all to you. In clear, understandable language. I didn't want to get involved, I said. I'm not interested in a relationship, I said.

"I want to experience *life*." She could feel her face flush with heated emotion. "And no one is going to keep me from it. Glory, Delaware, has nothing to offer me. Absolutely nothing. I've lived every one of my twenty-three years in a desolate nowhere with nothing to offer. I *will not* trade one small town for another!"

She turned from him then and raced for the safety of the house.

Amy padded by the family room, where she heard the television playing softly. She should go in and check on the twins, say her good-nights, but she was physically trembling from having lied to Pierce so thoroughly and she didn't want the boys to see her in this state.

However, her steps slowed as she passed the doorway and then halted altogether when she heard her name being called. Funny how she could tell which child had spoken just by the sound of his voice. She hadn't needed to see Jeremiah's tiny scar to know who had called out to her.

She turned and paused in the family-room doorway. "Yes? I'm right here."

"Could you hand me my drink, please?" he asked, his voice low. "I can't reach it."

"Of course." She was surprised when she entered the dimly lit room and saw that both boys had moved from the floor, where their sleeping bags had been set up, to the couch. Benjamin was fast asleep, his head resting on Jeremiah's shoulder.

As she reached for the glass, she asked him, "Would you like me to move Benjamin to his sleeping bag?"

"Oh, no. We have a pact. If one of us falls asleep, the other is supposed to wake him up. This movie is almost over, so I thought I'd let him rest until it was time for the next show."

He grasped the glass and took a drink. "Thanks." He handed it over and she put it back on the table.

Amy noticed that Jeremiah had quenched his thirst while keeping his shoulders as still as possible.

"It's good to have someone to lean on," the child innocently observed.

A flash of heartrending emotion had her blinking back stinging tears.

"When Mommy and Daddy first talked about going to Africa," he continued, "they thought that Mommy should stay here with us. But me and Benjamin talked about it. We didn't like thinking that Daddy would be all alone. My brother and me have each other. Daddy needed to have someone, too. He was going to be an awfully long way from home."

The knot that had formed in her throat made it

difficult to speak. "You're a good brother, Jeremiah. And a good son, too."

"Benjamin would let me lean my head on him if I got tired. That's what's so good about having someone, ya know?"

A scalding tear welled and slipped silently down her cheek. She swiped at it quickly and sniffed. She didn't answer him. She simply couldn't.

Movement at the threshold of the room made her lift her gaze. Pierce's green eyes were on her. She knew from his expression that he'd heard the entire exchange...had witnessed her emotional response.

She tried to guess what he was feeling. Hurt, that much was clear from the turbulent shadows clouding his gaze. But he was bewildered, as well. Why, he probably wondered, did she find a little boy's ramblings so heartrending when she'd just made a hard-line declaration that no one and nothing would keep her from her dreams?

She'd led Pierce to believe that it was her quest for adventure, for life experiences, that was keeping her from having a relationship with him. That was a lie, plain and simple.

And she didn't like the feeling the fib churned up in her. It wasn't who she was...or who she wanted to be.

Perception be damned.

He deserved the truth. Even if it meant his opinion of her would completely change.

Amy straightened her spine, and then she approached Pierce.

"Can I talk to you in your study? There's something you need to know."

His mouth, the one that had been so pliant, so pleasurable when he'd kissed her, was pursed tight. She feared he might refuse, but then he offered her a single stiff nod before stalking off toward the study.

Never before had she cared so much about what someone might think of her. She'd realized out there by the bay that she loved this man. With every fiber of her being.

But wasn't that just her luck? To discover she'd lost her heart to a man at the very moment she was going to have to tell him the truth about herself? A truth that would leave him disappointed, disillusioned and dismayed.

With leaden feet she followed him down the hall.

When she entered the study she saw that Pierce had gone to the bar. He reached over the wine bottle and went straight for the Scotch. He poured two fingers of the amber liquid into a crystal highball glass before turning to face her.

"Would you like a drink?"

"No." Her reasoning needed to be fully sober if she was going to tell him her story without breaking down like a crybaby. Keeping her humiliation to a minimum would be the best she could hope for at this point.

The wood of the door was cool against her fingertips as she closed it and moved farther into the room. She moistened her lips, her chest expanding in a nerve-steeling inhalation.

"I have a confession to make." The deep breath she'd just taken did little to quiet the butterflies that fluttered furiously in the pit of her belly.

He didn't say a word, just stood across the room staring at her.

"I—I wasn't…quite truthful with you," she began, the words coming with excruciating slowness, "out there…tonight."

Tension forced her to swallow, but her dry throat made the effort difficult. She looked away from him, spending an inordinate amount of energy on crossing the room and settling herself on the leather sofa in order to avoid his verdant stare.

Her eyes latched onto the blown-glass paperweight on the table in front of her. "I explained to you early on how I felt about relationships, about marriage, about children. How I felt they were traps that would keep me from achieving my dreams of seeing whatever was outside my tiny hometown of Lebo. I felt as if I might as well shrivel up and die if I had to remain in Kansas for the rest of my life."

She saw how her fingers had laced themselves tightly in her lap. Her knees and ankles were pressed together and her spine was straight as she perched on the edge of the couch.

"I told you how I had watched as my friends settled down, one after an other, and had families. And how I felt their choices forever entangled them in dull and monotonous lives. And how I never, ever wanted that for myself.

"Well—" her brow furrowed "—my time here with the boys, with you, has taught me quite a lot about…well, about life. Being with the three of you these past weeks has made me adjust my thinking."

The urge to look him in the face welled up, but she simply couldn't bring herself to do it just yet.

"I—I've come to the conclusion that all those friends of mine, the ones who found…"

Love, she nearly said.

"The ones who found husbands, the ones who had children…I believe they all knew something that I didn't." Her sigh was shaky, and she was oh-so-careful to keep her eyes lowered. "And that realization has so much to do with what Jeremiah had to say in there just now.

"All this time…" Her tone took on a dreamlike quality, as if she were working this out, speaking to no one but herself, and that somehow made the task easier. "I've had this idea that out there, somewhere, *anywhere* other than where I was, I would find this nebulous excitement that I craved. But being here—" *with you* "—has taught me that anyplace can be an exciting paradise filled with unimaginable adventure."

The room felt utterly still, and although her logical mind screamed at her to keep her eyes off Pierce, she couldn't prevent her chin from rising, couldn't stop her gaze from searching for and finding his face.

Oh, Lord. Rather than acknowledging what her time here had taught her, she should have gone ahead and confessed her truth. Judging from the light in his eyes, her revelation had succeeded only in planting a seed of hope in him. And it was swiftly sprouting.

Frowning, she shook her head slowly, and the brightness in his gaze faded. Amy felt as if she'd stomped on his budding hope. It had to be done. There was no avoiding it.

Anguish nicked her heart with painful pinpricks.

"There are things about me, Pierce. Things you

don't know. Things that would change your opinion of me. You don't know me. I'm not—'' Apprehension had her throat muscles hitching. ''I'm not the person you think I am.''

He set his drink on the side table and rounded the chair that had separated them.

''This is about *you?*'' He sounded quite shocked. ''I thought this was about me. That there was something wrong with me. That there was something about me you detested.''

''*What?*'' She couldn't keep the surprise out of her voice. Then her tone softened as she added, ''You're perfect, Pierce. Perfect in every way.''

Knowing that she'd revealed too much, Amy was astonished when he didn't react to her compliment.

He sat down next to her, but he didn't touch her. ''There's nothing you could tell me, Amy, that would change how I feel about you.''

Panic set in. ''Please know that I never intended you to learn about my past. I *like* the Amy you think I am. I like what I see when you look at me. The truth will change that. I can tell from the expression in your eyes that you think I'm capable and competent and strong and smart—''

His hands were warm when they took hold of hers. His grip was firm, and her body flushed with heat.

''You *are* the Amy I think you are. How could you be anything else? I've gotten to know you. I've seen you with the boys. You've loved them, cared for them, laughed with them, taught them. You've helped me take care of them. You've cared for me. You've helped me with my work. You've cared enough about me to force me to change my thinking about myself. Even when I was angry with you for doing it.''

It would have been so easy to lose herself in the depths of those soulful eyes of his, to drown in them. But that would be a mistake.

''You are capable and competent and strong and smart. You're an amazing woman, Amy. I've already told you that's how I feel. I can't believe you'd think anything else about yourself.''

Her heart wrenched. She had to end this. And she had to do it now.

''I'm not the woman for you. You have to believe me.'' She tried to pull her hands free, but he held fast.

She could hear her pulse pounding as she lifted her gaze to his.

''I've never met a woman like you.'' His voice wrapped around her like a silken scarf. ''I don't plan to let you go easily.''

With the rounding of her spine, her spirit slumped. Tucking her chin to her chest, she whispered, ''Y-you're the smartest person I've ever met, Pierce. I—I'm not your intellectual equal. I'm not self-assured, or proficient at anything. I'm not—''

''What are you talking about? You were so proficient that you had me quaking in my boots when you first arrived.''

''Perception.'' She whispered the word, then closed her eyes. ''My instructor in flight attendant school drilled into me that perception is everything. It was there, during my training stint, that I created the Amy who is sitting here beside you right now.''

This confession was stealing the very soul out of

her. Her tone got weaker with each sentence she spoke.

She couldn't look into his face. Oh, he was going to be so disappointed. He was going to be mortified that he'd ever touched her, kissed her, that he'd ever considered having a relationship with her. He was going to be angry with her for leading him to believe that she was something she was not.

"I don't understand."

Finally she could take the strain no longer. "I didn't finish school."

His brow furrowed, then he looked relieved. "Is that all? Lots of people don't finish college, Amy. Cynthia didn't. She met John when he was invited to speak at her campus, they fell in love and she quit school to get married. This is no big deal. In fact, lots of people don't attend a single college course."

"High school. I didn't finish high school."

It was clear that the notion had never entered his head. "B-but how can that be? You speak French. You've taught the boys to count. You helped me translate that letter."

"I dabble in what, to me, is a romantic language. I listen to audiotapes and recite what I hear. It's no more complicated than that."

He must have realized that he'd sounded accusatory. "I wasn't judging you."

"It's okay. I understand." This time when she attempted to pull her hands from his, she succeeded. Well, she decided miserably, at least the finality of it all was sinking into his head. He was letting her go. If not consciously, then at least on a subliminal level.

"How could something like this happen in this day and age?" he asked.

She lifted one shoulder in a slight shrug. "A couple of months into my senior year, my father contracted pneumonia. He was very ill. We couldn't afford to hire more help, so I took some time off school to keep the motel running. Weeks turned into months. And just when I thought I was going to go back, Dad had a relapse. This time his hospital stay was two full weeks. The illness took its toll. Dad's stamina never returned. I just didn't feel I could leave him to go back and get my diploma."

Reaching out, he curled his index finger under her chin and tipped up her face.

"Amy, you said before that your father had sacrificed so much for you. That he'd done everything in his power to keep you with him."

She searched his green eyes, feeling breathless.

"I think you need to give yourself a little more credit. You've made quite a sacrifice yourself."

Her cheeks tinged pink. "I did it because...well, because we had to keep the business going. I love my dad. And that business was everything to him." After a short pause, she said, "I do know what I've forfeited. That's why I've been so adamant about my life goals. I wanted my turn. I felt I deserved it."

The silence grew awkward for her, but Pierce looked relaxed, comfortable in it as he contemplated something...what exactly, she couldn't say. All she was cognizant of was her embarrassment. When she'd arrived here, she'd never imagined she'd be telling Pierce the truth about her uneducated state. She'd been looked down upon by a great number of people in her lifetime; however, she hadn't fallen in love with any of them.

"What were you when all this happened—"

The question baffled her.

"Seventeen? Eighteen?" he clarified. Evidently he wasn't looking for an answer from her, but instead plowed ahead with his thoughts. "You were a teenager, taking care of your sick father and running a business. You nursed your father. And the business succeeded well enough that a major hotel chain offered to buy you out."

Again the suffocating quiet covered them and she felt as if she wanted to gasp for air.

"I think," Pierce said at last, "that your accomplishments make you pretty damned capable, pretty damned strong and pretty damned smart."

Sometime during his speech he'd taken hold of her hand again. She hadn't a clue when that had been. Amy felt as if she'd had the wind knocked out of her. She'd expected him to be appalled by the truth. Disgusted by her lack of education. Most people were.

"I love you, Amy. I've seen your sharp mind at work. I've seen your caring nature. I want you to marry me. I want you to have my children."

She couldn't believe her ears. How could he suggest such an outrageous notion?

"That can't happen!" she blurted, ire and humiliation flaring. "What would we tell our children, Pierce? Daddy is smart enough to create something that no one else could even conceive of. Mommy, on the other hand, wasn't able to finish high school."

The mere idea of explaining her past to sweet and innocent babies she and Pierce might create threw her into a complete tailspin. However, through the panicky miasma came a slow and arduous realization. *The man who has stolen your heart has just professed that he loves you, that he wants you to be his wife.*

Even though you've told him the humiliating truth.

How could he want her? When he knew all the things she was not?

She hadn't expected this, and the bewilderment she felt had her falling speechless. But he didn't seem the least put off by her silence.

"A person doesn't need a piece of paper to define who they are, Amy," he said.

"That's easy for you to say. All you have to do is look up on the wall there at all your degrees and diplomas."

He gave her hand a gentle squeeze, slid close enough that their thighs were pressed tightly together.

"All those traits you thought you created…"

A tone isn't something that Amy ever imagined would have texture and form, but his voice contained a quality somewhat akin to liquid gold. It flowed over her, through her, filling her with an array of conflicting emotions that ricocheted and collided like an explosion of fireworks.

"Well, you've always had those characteristics in you. They've always been a part of who you are. If you hadn't possessed them, no amount of acting would have conjured them up."

Amy studied his face, his eyes. Hard. Could it be that his faith in her was stronger than the misery of her past?

"I—I," she stammered, "don't know what to say."

"Say you love me."

He believed in her!

When she didn't respond immediately, he repeated, "Say you love me."

Oh, she did! Pure elation surged through her. But then darker emotions made a fierce attack.

Tears of anguish made her vision go blurry. "B-but if we *were* to have…"

Children was the word she couldn't get her tongue to utter. The idea of having Pierce's children was still so amazingly foreign to her that she couldn't quite wrap her mind around it. But he knew what she was referring to—she could tell from the way his expression softened.

"What on earth would we tell them? How could I ever explain—"

"The truth." He cut her off with a smile that was tender. "The truth is always best."

Distress rounded her shoulders. "But my truth is horrible."

He placed a quieting finger against her lips. "Honey, you've been looking at the truth from the wrong angle. From where I see it, you're a caring, sacrificing, enterprising, simply amazing woman. Those are all things instilled in a person at birth. Perception has nothing to do with it."

He wrapped his arm around her then, and with his free hand he lifted her face with the lightest of touches until their gazes met, locked.

"I'm still waiting."

The adoration reflected in his clear green eyes chased away all her doubt and worry. She knew what he was waiting for, and she didn't intend to delay a moment longer.

"I love you so much, Pierce—" her voice was thick with all she was feeling "—that it hurts my heart."

He kissed her then, and every argument logic had ever conjured up regarding idiots and intellects was silenced by the love he showered on her. He believed in her. He thought she was strong and competent and wise. And best of all, he had convinced her to believe all these things about herself.

She would love this man for all eternity.

Epilogue

There was nothing like spring in Paris. Unless, of course, it was spring on the French Riviera. For the life of her, Amy couldn't decide which was more beautiful. Or more exciting.

However, the most exhilarating experience to date had to be the afternoon, not ten short days ago, that she had become Pierce's wife.

The wedding had been a glorious affair. Right there on the banks of the Delaware Bay she and Pierce had vowed to love each other through all eternity. Her white gown had billowed like puffy clouds as her father had led her to her betrothed. Pierce had looked gorgeous in his black tux. The twins had participated by carrying the rings, each boy balancing a satin pillow as they walked the length of the grassy aisle. Cynthia had acted as her matron of honor. Family and friends had offered the newlywed couple a standing ovation as Reverend John Winthrop had pronounced them Dr. and Mrs. Pierce Kincaid.

Her wedding day had been the most joyous of Amy's life.

But then came the honeymoon, and Pierce had surprised her with a trip to France.

The City of Light had bustled with tourists and Parisians alike. Amy and Pierce had visited the Arc de Triomphe, the Eiffel Tower and the Louvre. And they had whiled away long afternoons in the brasseries, the quaint little cafés that served strong cappuccino and those lusciously rich pastries that were sure to have her gaining weight.

After almost a week in Paris they had flown to Nice, a sizable city on the Mediterranean. They had rented a car and had driven in one direction to Canne and Juan-les-Pins, then in the other direction to a picturesque town called Villefranche-sur-Mer. And today they had explored Menton, a small French village from which the lush Italian countryside could be seen in a distance.

"Tired?"

Concern shadowed Pierce's gem-green eyes, and Amy smiled as she stretched out under the cool sheets.

"Exhausted," she told him.

He smoothed the backs of his fingers down her bare shoulder, and desire quickened in her...desire so sharp that she nearly gasped.

"Maybe we should turn out the lights and get some rest."

Her smile widened slowly, languorously. "Oh, we'll turn out the lights, all right. But there'll be no resting for quite a while yet."

The corners of his mouth pulled back into a sexy grin, his gaze darkening with yearning.

"I am so glad to hear you say that."

He buried his face against her neck, his husky growl sending shivers coursing across her skin. She chuckled then, infusing a throaty quality into it that she knew he'd find alluring.

"What?" he asked, rising onto his elbow to gaze down into her face. "What are you thinking?"

"Oh, I was just remembering how, when we first met, I was so attracted to your brain."

His brows rose a fraction. "My brain?"

"You were so intelligent that I thought it was sexy."

He laughed. "I don't like how you phrased that in the past tense."

"Oh, you know what I mean." She reached up and combed her fingers through his hair. "But I've been learning, sir, that you're more than just clever." Passion flared, expressing itself in her seductive gaze. "You're a man of many talents."

She cradled his face between her hands, pulled him to her and planted a sweltering kiss on his mouth.

Long moments later he smiled at her. "I do aim to please."

Her pulse chugged, her heart thudded with need. Her voice came out sounding raspy as she proclaimed, "I know you do."

To think that Amy had run from what she'd thought was the trap of marriage, the pitfall of family, the hazards of the heart. And here she was, encoun-

tering some of the most awesome excitement the
world had to offer while basking in the greatest experience of all....

The love of a lifetime.

* * * * *

If you enjoyed what you just read,
then we've got an offer you can't resist!

Take 2 bestselling love stories FREE!

Plus get a FREE surprise gift!

SILHOUETTE *Romance*®

Who will marry the boss's daughter?

Wintersoft's CEO is on a husband hunt for his daughter. Trouble is Emily has uncovered his scheme. Can she marry off the eligible executives in the company before Dad sets his crazy plan in motion?

Love, Your Secret Admirer by SUSAN MEIER
(on sale September 2003)

Her Pregnant Agenda by LINDA GOODNIGHT
(on sale October 2003)

Fill-in Fiancée by DeANNA TALCOTT
(on sale November 2003)

Santa Brought a Son by MELISSA McCLONE
(on sale December 2003)

Rules of Engagement by CARLA CASSIDY
(on sale January 2004)

One Bachelor To Go by NICOLE BURNHAM
(on sale February 2004)

With office matchmakers on the loose, is any eligible executive safe?

Available at your favorite retail outlet.

Silhouette®
Where love comes alive™

Visit Silhouette at www.eHarlequin.com   SRMTBD

COMING NEXT MONTH

#1702 RULES OF ENGAGEMENT—Carla Cassidy
Marrying the Boss's Daughter

Nate Leeman worked best alone, yet Wintersoft's senior VP
now found himself the reluctant business partner to computer
guru—and ex-girlfriend—Kat Sanderson. The hunky executive
knew business and pleasure didn't mix. So why was he suddenly looking forward to long hours and late nights with his capti-
vating co-worker?·

#1703 THE BACHELOR BOSS—Julianna Morris

Sweet virgin Libby Dumont's former flame was now her
boss? She'd shared one far-too-intimate kiss with the confirmed
bachelor a decade ago, and although Neil O'Rourke was as
handsome as ever, she knew he must remain off-limits. She
just had to focus on business—*not* Neil's knee-weakening kisses!

#1704 BABY, OH BABY!—Teresa Southwick
If Wishes Were…

When Rachel Manning spoke her secret wish—to have a
baby—she never expected to become an instant mother. She
didn't even have a boyfriend! Yet here she was, temporary parent for a sweet month-old infant. Until Jake Fletcher—
the baby's take-charge, heartbreaker-in-a-Stetson-and-jeans
uncle—showed up and suggested sharing more than late-night
feedings….

#1705 THE BABY CHRONICLES—Lissa Manley

Aiden Forbes was in trouble! He hadn't seen Colleen Stewart
since she walked out on him eight years ago. Now he had
been teamed with the marriage-shy journalist to photograph
an article on babies, and seeing Colleen surrounded by all
these adorable infants was giving Aiden ideas about a baby
of their own!

SRCNM1203